GW00891803

Moonshine

An Anthology by the Warwick Writing Programme

Ball Bearing Press

Moonshine
Copyright 2017 © An anthology from the Warwick MA in Writing 2017

https://mawanthology.wordpress.com

ISBN 978-0-9566700-9-0
First published in Great Britain by Ball Bearing Press

A catalogue record of this book is available from the British Library

Set and designed by The Book Refinery Ltd

Cover Design by Jason Tse

Contents

Contents

Foreword

In Britain today emerging writers face an apparently ever-darker future. Publishing houses seem increasingly impervious to new voices, passing on their impregnability to agents. The self-publishing model is increasingly offered as a solution to the market's problems, with the author expected to provide both content and the funds for production costs. And yet - of course - voices still struggle to be heard, still burn with a remarkable innocence, still battle to learn, improve and transform inspiration into lucidity. As a professor working within the Warwick Writing Programme I have the privilege to watch each year as the processes of discovery and refinement take place, as fresh realities are made. At a time when so much appears to be dark in the wider world, when creativity is so often denied and when our younger generations are expected to bear so many burdens I am heartened by the continuing ingenuity and tenacity of the students who come to us. This anthology is the work of our full- and part-time MA students.

It's no surprise that there is darkness here and threat. There are loved children, but there are dead children. The glitz and wealth of Canary Wharf is haunted by the dead, visceral experiences of personal destruction. An Antarian observer studies humanity - animalistic, feral and yet passionate, remarkable, individual. He ponders animal rights for the Antarian's stock of imported humans, while living in an urban wasteland we humans might find familiar. In one quietly touching story a child collects bullets in Bethlehem on the day his world explodes. Here an uncanny man in black pursues an innocent narrator, there police tinker with the wording of their report on a suicide, before strange evidence emerges. In a quietly melancholy and humane piece, an apartment block's residents are brought together by the plunging death of a stranger in Armani. And, in a deftly understated piece, an abusive relationship begins to take its toll on a trapped wife.

Still, there is humour, too. Political satire winds through a tale of genital tasering and al fresco sex. Wisecracking observations accompany an alien mission that lands on an earth with bright promises for Homo sapiens: a singularly unpromising species.

There are the songs of despair here, loss and depression, but also of their resistance. A witch lays out the lyricism of her strange triumphs. Liverpool is post-industrial, but still has Liver Birds and dreams of music - and a sense of humour... And there is love: gay love, straight love, family love, complicated love, unrequited love, forbidden love, love of nature, of details, of words and their promises and of life. These are writers enjoying their exploration of 'haunted' words.

While one author warns us *"Things of dark imagining were coming, drawn by the sound of her voice."* another offers us the ambivalent reassurance that *"There was no emptiness that time could not snow its way into."* These are writers feeling their way towards a deeper and deeper understanding of life in an age that has - in high places and low - rejected understanding. But these voices are in it for the duration and proceeding with wary hope and a sense of the necessity of beauty.

The idea of Moonshine carries a little poetry, a little light, a certain risk in brewing something illicit at home. The intoxicant offered here is the good stuff, hooch with a kick. And it owes something to the swirl of enchanted visions that sweep through '*A Midsummer Night's Dream*'. You'll remember that's the play in which a weaver calls out, full of artistic passion and simple joy, *"Find out moonshine! Find out moonshine!"* And then he is enchanted. It's a fit and proper thing for an anthology to promise altered states and odd transformations - that's what writing is supposed to deliver.

The Warwick Writing Programme is a sincere creation of writers and academics. It brings together teaching, inspiration and provocation designed to help new writing and new writers thrive - it would be nothing without its students.

This anthology gives you a series of insights into the persistent life of art and creative thought, both in the UK and around the world. I imagine it telling you, along with one narrator - *I wish you a full life, and luck against your own monsters - A. L. Kennedy*

The Alien Ambassador

Kai Wang

(A novel extract)

Aliens offer humanity the cure for cancer.
But everything has a price.

In his twenty-eight years of life, Issac Turner had learned that there was nothing more resolute than a moron who had made up his mind. Nothing could budge a moron who was convinced – especially if others had told him that he was righteous.

Come up with a three-word, three-syllable chant and you can conquer the world.

Yes we can.

Lock her up.

Screw them all.

Chapter 1

Issac raced across the vinyl hospital floor. His breathing was rapid. His eyes filled with blind urgency. In his hands he clutched a small orange bottle containing a single red pill.

'Room twenty-eight...' He glanced left and right. Twenty...twenty-five – there it was. He burst into room twenty-eight without knocking.

A dying woman lay on a bed, her body linked up to a heart rate monitor, her brittle arms skewered with IV needles. Cancer had ravaged her body; her hair was gone, her face gaunt, the kindness in her eyes a fleeting shadow of what she once was. Issac stopped in his tracks. For a moment, he did not recognise her; this sight of her did not match with any of his memories from many years ago.

'Mother,' Issac said.

Next to her bed sat a young woman — his sister. It was the first time he had seen her in almost ten years. She turned to him. She said nothing.

'Eve.' Issac nodded in her direction. She acknowledged him with a scowl. He sat down, not noticing the doctor who stood in a corner. The doctor glanced at his watch. That woman should be dead before dinner.

'Mother, it's me,' Issac said and held her hand.

He watched the old woman slowly turn her head to him. Her eyes were unfocused, but their corners crinkled when she met his gaze.

'Issac,' she whispered in a quiet voice, soft like the last summer breeze at the beginning of autumn.

He wanted to apologise for not coming sooner, apologise for all the years he had not called her, or visited her, like a good son would have done. But he did not utter those apologies; they were redundant at this point. He knew it, she knew it; he had taken her existence for granted and never given her needs a second thought. He had countless excuses to ward away the guilt.

Either way, this was the end.

'Issac, take care of your sister once I'm gone.' She rested her hand on his. It was lighter than a feather.

He nodded. He swallowed a lump in his throat.

'Eve...' The girl peered at her mother and saw only an abyss. 'Make sure Issac eats properly...he always forgets to eat when he works...he's always been like that.'

Eve wiped away her tears and nodded weakly.

'Issac, remember to put on thick socks in the winter...you get the flu so easily…' She coughed and it seemed that her body might fall apart.

There was a pause. A silent breath.

'Eve…make sure to eat your vegetables…'

A weak cough.

'Issac…visit your sister…she misses you…'

She closed her eyes. Her expression was at peace. She had not died yet, but Issac did not have to be a doctor to know.

'Eve…can I have a moment alone with Mother, please?'

He felt her indignant glare, the accusation in it, but he did not care.

'Fine,' she said. She and the doctor exited the room.

When the door closed, Issac got up and glanced about to make sure that he was truly alone. Good. There were no security cameras. He opened the little plastic bottle and the red pill landed in the palm of his hand.

He turned to his mother. There was no way that she could swallow something of this size. It would have to be injected directly into her blood. He quickly rummaged through the cupboards, always glancing at the door, afraid that someone would come in. There it was – a syringe. He mashed the red pill into powder, mixed it with a little water and sucked it up into the syringe. He swallowed his trepidation. This had to work. Without fail. He injected the red fluid into the IV injection port.

His mother took a deep breath. She did not open her eyes.

He exited the room. He had somewhere else to be.

'Issac?' Eve said. 'Where are you going?'

'I have to get back to work.'

'W-what?' Complete and utter disbelief. 'Mom is going to die! The doctor just told me that she isn't going to make it through the day! And – and you're going –'

'I have to go.'

'Fine, go. I'll deal with all this. You get back to the office to do whatever you do. Go!'

He knew that his sister would never forgive him. But his work here was done. There were other matters to attend to. Time was running out.

Chapter 2

Dribble slowly. Speed up. Fake to the right, crossover to the left, then a quick behind-the-back dribble to switch to the right, then crossover to the left again. The guard should be confused if the execution was fast enough.

Issac burst through the gap on the left. The defence had not anticipated this. He took the ball in his hands, ready to make a hook-shot.

Too early. The centre guard towered over him, his fingertips grazing the ball just as it left Issac's right hand. The ball lost its momentum and hit the edge of the basket. The ball went to the opponent.

Two minutes later, Issac had lost the game. Three-nil.

'What's wrong with you, man?' Sam Wiseman sat down and passed Issac a warm Gatorade. They sat on the outside benches, watching other players on the outdoor court. It was a two-on-two rotation tournament; whichever team lost would get switched out.

'We didn't score a single point. Your game isn't focused!' Sam said, wiping his face with a towel. 'You keep passing to the wrong player. Whose side are you on?'

Issac listened intently, nodding. There was a wistful smile on his lips, but he was not upset about the loss. He stared at the players on the court. He listened to the screeching sound of sudden stops. The dribble. The shouting. The whooshing sound of a clean three-pointer.

'I'm sorry,' Issac said simply.

Sam sighed. 'We'll win next time.'

Issac said nothing. He took a gulp of his Gatorade and walked over to one of the free baskets. Sam followed him, thinking that he wanted to play a one-on-one. Instead, Issac stood right under the basket, staring up at it. Then he stroked the metal pole which held the basket high in the air. He put his forehead against the cool metal surface, taking in all the scents of the basketball court.

'Hey, are you alright?' Sam asked.

'Yeah.'

'You're acting like you're dying.'

Issac smiled slightly. 'Sam, tell me one thing.'

'Sure. What?'

'If everyone called me the world's most evil murderer…a demon, a monster…pure evil; if they said that I killed millions of people, would you still be my friend?'

Sam opened his mouth to answer, but said nothing.

'Sam?' Issac's voice had no humour in it. His eyes were glazed with a peculiar hardness.

Sam laughed nervously. 'What are you talking about, man? You know it's impossible for you to kill millions of people…'

'Hitler did it, Stalin did it, Mao did it.'

'Yeah, but they didn't literally kill millions. They used other people to execute their policies and so on.'

'Just answer me.'

'Man, what's wrong with you these days?'

'Nothing.'

Chapter 3

There was no warning. They simply arrived on a Tuesday night. Right after the NBA finals and right before the Premier League games.

It hovered above the United Nations Headquarters in downtown Manhattan, ominously, silent as death. It was oval-shaped, smooth, slim and made from grey metal — minimalistic, elegant, transcending all ambiguity.

The games were stopped. No point in broadcasting something no-one will watch. The world turned off Netflix and turned on the news for once. School was cancelled. Trading at the New York Stock Exchange dried to a trickle. Money never sleeps, but the presence of aliens certainly slows it down.

What do they want? Why are they here? Had dialogue been established?

#Aliens trended at #1 on Twitter, Facebook and Instagram.

Later, Google would report that for about three hours, every search query that was entered into its search engine – billions upon billions – contained the words 'Alien', 'UFO', or 'Death'. After three hours, people began googling 'iPhone', 'Justin Bieber' and 'Am I pregnant?' again.

The White House was evacuated. Jets were scrambled. Every military of every country was placed on high alert. American aircraft carriers, tiny nutshells when compared to the UFO, were positioned off the east and west coast.

Some people tried to run out of the city. Some tried to run in.

Some screamed that it was God's punishment, others screamed that it was God's reward. They all held the same Bible.

Why are they here?

Then a single tweet exploded on Twitter. It came from the Twitter handle *@twhstory*. It said:

We have arrived.

And then fifteen minutes later:

We ask President Child for a conference room at the United Nation Headquarters. 1 week from now. #pressconference

Chapter 4

Issac struggled with his tie. It had been years since he had put on one of these. As soon as he had been promoted to an upper management position, he'd stopped wearing ties for good. At least, that was what he thought at the time.

'Do you need help?' someone asked.

'I think I can figure this out.'

After another ten minutes, the tie was perfect, just reaching his belt.

Issac turned to his assistant – a man wearing a tailored suit, holding an iPad in his hands. Issac couldn't tell what his expression and age were because the man didn't have a face, only a full head of hair.

'What do you think?' he asked.

The man shrugged. His shoulders moved mechanically as though this movement was unnatural to him.

Issac sighed and turned back to the mirror. 'We have arrived...' Issac mumbled. 'We have arrived. Yeah, no shit you have arrived.'

In response, the Faceless Man readied the iPad and began to type a response. Moments later a message appeared on the other iPad which Issac had next to him on a table. He read the message. 'Twitter seems to be the dominant platform for announcements on this planet.'

Issac laughed softly, mockingly.

'One thing I don't understand though,' Issac said while buttoning his suit, 'out of the billions of tweets, how come your single Tweet exploded?'

The Faceless Man typed a response. Again, the message was sent to

Issac's tablet. 'The United Nations HQ Wi-Fi has a unique frequency and IP address. When we parked over the building, we hacked into the Wi-Fi signal and sent the Tweet. Then someone at Twitter HQ picked it up.'

'Hah!' Issac laughed. 'You can literally travel at the speed of light, but you don't have Wi-Fi on your ship.'

He walked over to the living room table and picked up a small orange bottle with a red pill inside. 'Well, let's go.'

The Faceless Man nodded. His body trembled, bones creaked and groaned and his suit vanished. He became a black mass of matter. Then he split into five pieces, each forming itself into a faceless muscled bodyguard.

'Right.' Issac took a deep breath and stepped towards the door. He put his hand on the door handle and stopped. 'One more thing. I don't think people will find you trustworthy – not without faces. Would you mind putting one on?'

The faceless bodyguards appeared confused, but Issac couldn't be sure given they were faceless. Noses, eyes, and lips appeared.

'You forgot the ears.'

Ears popped out from their heads.

'I think that's good enough.'

Chapter 5

United Nations Press Conference Room. 10:00am Eastern Standard Time.

Entering the United Nations building in New York wasn't much of a problem. When Issac and his five bodyguards descended from the space ship, they landed on the rooftop. An escort of the most experienced

Secret Service agents surrounded him and ushered him inside. His five alien bodyguards followed.

An hour later, Issac stood at the podium where world leaders usually stood. The press room was rather small for the purposes, so every country was only allowed to send one reporter. In the back of the room were several large cameras, broadcasting to the rest of the world.

'Good morning, everyone,' Issac said. He smiled slightly. Remember to smile. People trust a man who smiles with sincerity. 'My name is Issac Turner. I have been appointed by the aliens as their ambassador. I will act as the channel of communication between them and the human race.'

He reached into his breast pocket and took out two passports. 'Before anyone asks, I am a one-hundred-percent genuine human being. I am a dual American-New Zealand citizen. I pay my taxes and hate the IRS as much as you do. I have a Masters degree. My high school girlfriend broke my heart.'

There were a few chuckles in the room. Good, Issac thought, letting out a silent breath. First humanise yourself and make clear that you are on their side and then drop the big thing.

One reporter raised her hand. She was blonde, tall and beautiful. She spoke with a French accent. Perhaps the French Prime Minister hoped that Isaac would take a liking to her and give France special treatment. 'Yes?'

'Monique Duprat, AFP. Mr Turner, why are they here? What do they want from us?'

Issac smiled. Not a threatening smile, a wistful smile. This is it.

'They want nothing from us,' Issac answered. 'In fact, they want to give us something.' After a short pause he added: 'Something wonderful.'

Nobody said anything. The tension in the room was so thick that he could taste it.

He reached into his inner breast pocket and pulled out the small orange bottle. He took out the red pill and held it between his fingers. Photographers forgot to take pictures.

'Ladies and gentlemen, it is my privilege to announce the cure for cancer. This little red pill will eliminate any kind of cancer. It is the result of years of research by the aliens and now they are ready to give it to us.' He paused. 'But there are a few requirements that need to be fulfilled first.'

Fear. That was the first emotion Issac saw in their eyes. The cold hand of dread in their guts. The feeling a child would have when their father was morosely drunk.

'The aliens will give us the cure for cancer if we agree to certain terms that they propose.'

Issac took a breath. He was more nervous than he thought he would be. He was about to make an announcement that would rock the world. In the back of his mind he wondered if he would have a chance to sleep with this Monique woman from AFP. He chuckled inwardly. To him, this was proof that he was still human.

'The aliens will give us the cure for cancer if we sign an agreement on open borders and free trade with them.'

A moment of silence. And then –

The room erupted.

'Right! If we agree to this, they will give us the cure for cancer,' Issac shouted above the torrent of questions. 'That is all! Further details will be announced after a discussion with world leaders.'

Chapter 6

Outside the press room, the Secret Service escorted Issac and his alien bodyguards down a set of stairs, to a meeting room that was fifty feet underground, sealed by ten feet of solid concrete and another five inches of steel plates. It was the most secure location on the continent. The Americans believed it to be the most secure location in the world.

But Issac knew better. The most secure location was in orbit.

The meeting room itself was rather barren: a solid oak desk that stretched down for sixty feet, plus leather seats, and some basic snacks on the table: biscuits, water, orange juice. A toilet was in the back. The world's safest place to take a shit.

Over a hundred world leaders, national representatives and a few members of Congress and Parliament had gathered here; they were all waiting for the Alien Ambassador.

Issac sat down at the end of the table that was closest to the door. The metal door locked behind him. He glanced about; at the age of twenty-eight, he was without a doubt the youngest person present. President Child was in his second-term and seventy-five years old. Germany's Chancellor was fifty. The British Prime Minister was around sixty. Each leader had two bodyguards standing behind them.

'Mr Turner, welcome.' President Child stood. 'We appreciate you coming down here to meet us.'

Issac nodded. First get the formalities out of the way. There was a tough road ahead. 'Thank you for having me. It's an honour to be the representative.'

Before President Child or anyone else could speak, Issac continued.

'I believe that it is best for me to explain how my communication with the aliens will be conducted before we proceed with negotiations.'

All the world leaders were listening. Issac wondered if the world would be this united ever again.

'While I may not know all the reasons for the way they do things, the aliens have been communicating with me via a translation app written for the iPad.'

He took out his tablet. Behind him, one of his bodyguards took out a similar one.

'Usually when I speak, this thing records my voice with the voice dictation feature and the translation app then translates my speech into their written language and the translation will appear on their side.' Issac pointed at his bodyguard behind him.

'And when they want to talk to me, they write something on their tablet and a written translation appears on my side. I can use the voice dictation feature to have the message read out loud.'

That was the end of the explanation. 'If you have any questions, as I'm sure you do, please simply ask and I will do my best to answer.'

He crossed his fingers and set his hands on the table. There. He thought that he had said all of that in a friendly and approachable manner. Hopefully this would lead to smooth negotiations.

'Thank you, Mr Turner,' said President Child. 'We appreciate the information you have given us.'

Issac nodded. He noted that the man's voice had a slightly deferential tone to it – he probably reasoned that it was better to be too polite than too rude when dealing with a situation where few variables were fully known and understood. Issac was impressed; unlike some other men the Americans had voted into office, this man knew how to stay calm even in this strange situation.

'For security reasons, we have some questions regarding the way you communicate with the aliens. We want to clarify this to avoid any misunderstandings in the future.'

'Please, go on.'

President Child nodded at a man in a white lab coat sitting next to him. 'This is Professor Lawrence.'

Professor Lawrence stood. He cleared his throat. Round glasses and bald head. Shining grey eyes. Short stubble on his chin. Maybe around fifty-years-old, at the pinnacle of his career. Best in his field – whatever that was.

'Mr Turner,' Professor Lawrence said. 'This may seem trivial, but are the translations of your app one hundred percent accurate? We want to avoid any misunderstandings in our communications with the aliens as that could lead to disaster.'

'I assure you, they are correct. I have been communicating with the aliens with this app for almost a year and I am still alive.'

A few nervous smiles appeared around the room.

The professor continued. 'Am I right to assume that you wrote this translation app?'

'The app already existed when I came into contact with the aliens.'

'When and how did you come into contact with them?'

Issac smiled slightly. 'That is another story for another time.'

'How have the aliens come into possession of an iPad?'

Issac took out his wallet and produced a receipt. 'They ordered a pair of refurbished iPads at the Apple Store. They are surprisingly cost-conscious.'

Silence. Nobody laughed.

'Then I assume the aliens created this app?' Professor Lawrence continued.

Issac raised an eyebrow. That was a good question. He waited for an answer to appear on his iPad. An answer came. 'No, the aliens did not create this app.'

'Then who wrote it?'

A new message appeared on Issac's tablet. He read it out loud: 'We cannot comment on this matter at this time.'

Professor Lawrence and President Child exchanged nods. The professor sat down. Issac wondered if they wanted to press the matter further, but were afraid of showing even the slightest sign of disrespect.

Child stood again. He made a gesture and the woman sitting next to him got up. She looked about forty, had bobbed blonde hair, and wore an elegant black dress. Child said: 'May I introduce you to Susan Stedman. She will be the representative of the human race in all communications with the aliens.'

Issac half-opened his mouth. It dawned on him what was going on.

Behind him, his alien bodyguard typed a message. A translation appeared on Issac's end. He read it. He frowned. He then faced President Child.

'President Child...fellow leaders,' Issac began. 'I assume that you think that I am the ambassador who represents the aliens and Susan Stedman is the human representative, am I correct?'

'That is correct.'

'I will have to remind you that I am the one who has negotiated the deal with the aliens and that I am the only human being with whom the aliens communicate directly.' Issac swallowed the remainder of what he wanted to say: 'In other words, I am the sole channel of communication and I don't know what the hell this Stedman bitch is doing here.'

President Child and Susan Stedman sat down. A sharp tension rose in the room. No one wanted any conflict with the aliens – at least not yet.

Child cleared his throat. 'I believe that we can sort out the proper channels of communication at a later time. I think we are all in agreement that right now, the most urgent matter that needs to be discussed is the deal you have proposed at the press conference.'

'Please, ask all the questions you want. As far as I know, the aliens have no secrets.'

'What exactly do the aliens mean when you say that they want open borders and free trade in return for the cure for cancer?'

'Exactly that,' Issac said. 'They want to land on and leave the earth as they please, and they want to be able to buy and sell without restrictions. Simple as that. It doesn't have to be complicated.'

There was a short period of silence. 'Mr Turner, these terms are too vague and too broad. It will be impossible for us to agree to such a deal without knowing more details.'

'You are saying that such a move would be too drastic?'

There were several nods around the room.

Issac glanced down at his tablet and scrolled through his Twitter feed. The reaction of the general public was easy to gauge: confusion and fear.

Open borders and free trade. What does that even MEAN?

Will they colonise us?

Will aliens begin to live on our planet? This is our land! Property prices will only grow higher!

Issac frowned. No, this would not do.

'It seems that the announcement of the terms was handled in a rushed and unorganized manner,' Issac said. 'I will speak to the aliens and renegotiate. I will come back with more details in two weeks.'

Chapter 7

Exhausted, Issac dropped himself into the sofa chair. The press conference and talk with world leaders had been more tiring than he had anticipated; the tension in that room was unbearable. He had managed to keep a neutral expression the entire time, but he wasn't sure how long he could have kept it up.

For the first time, he felt glad to be back on the spaceship. The living area the Faceless Men had organised for him had always made him feel a little restless as the design of this space lacked something intangible — perhaps it was the human touch. But now, he was just happy to be away from all the pressure of the outside world.

He closed his eyes and took a deep breath. A new deal in two weeks. What to do? What did the Faceless Men have in mind? He opened one eye and glanced at his tablet. So far, the aliens had not sent him any new messages. Perhaps they were debating among themselves, or maybe even this period of waiting was part of their plan.

Issac shook his head. It didn't matter now. His stomach growled. He glanced about, his eyes taking on the gleam of a starved predator. Come to think of it, he thought, I've never had a meal up here before.

The living space itself was rather barren. There was an infinity window that allowed him to peer down onto New York City. There was a 4K television and a collection of sofas. Further back was a modern kitchen that had a stove, oven and fridge. The floor was stainless steel. It felt like a luxurious prison cell.

'Huh,' he murmured. That was new. When did a kitchen appear?

Food first. Questions later.

He stepped into the kitchen and opened the cupboards and fridge. Issac frowned. It was an IKEA kitchen; everything was clean and new, but there was no cooking equipment and the fridge was as empty as his stomach.

Issac picked up his tablet and wrote: 'Where is the food?'

Moments after he sent the message, the Faceless Man appeared before him. Where did he come from? Was he there the entire time watching Issac or was he somewhere else and had just materialised? Issac took a sharp breath, suppressing his surprise.

'Where is the food?' he asked again, pointing at the fridge.

'We didn't know your diet, so...' the Faceless Man wrote.

Issac waited for him to continue.

The Faceless Man produced a brown cloth bag that fitted snuggly into Issac's palm. It had considerable heft to it.

'What's this?' Issac asked.

'We wanted to wait until you moved in properly before we stocked the kitchen with food,' the Faceless Man said. 'This bag contains human currency that you can use to buy sustenance.'

Issac opened the bag and peered into it. He raised an eyebrow. 'How long have you had this for?'

The Faceless Man scratched his chin and appeared to think for a moment. Watching this motion disconcerted Issac. Scratching one's chin while thinking was a human thing.

'About two thousand years,' the Faceless Man answered.

Issac sighed. He reached into the bag and took out a gold coin. 'I don't think I can use this to buy anything.'

'Why not? All of our observations of your economy show that gold is always considered valuable.'

'The US went off the gold standard in 1971. Since then we have used fiat currencies.'

The Faceless Man said nothing.

Issac pulled out a green dollar bill and a credit card. 'Gold is still valuable and useful for investment and decorative purposes, but for the purchase of things, we use this.'

The Faceless Man shrugged. His shoulders creaked and groaned. Everything about his movement seemed unnatural. 'Suit yourself. Where do you want to be dropped off?'

Awakening

Steve Gay

(A novel extract)

The victim had been dead less than an hour. A forensic team was setting up in the downpour, huddling around the body in shining black capes, moving cases, adjusting instruments. A police detachment from downtown stood cradling their carbines, alloy heads turning in unison to scan the street. The rain hissed on the pavements, beat down on the victim's face, guttered along a vein raised thick as a cable on his cheek and still pulsing with the energy of the attack. The vein curled past his eye, drawing it open to expose a milky film, then buried itself between the horned scales of his forehead. And away to the side, opposite the pod station, a solitary kerb lamp flickered everything a tepid shade of green.

Gin D'Vani remembered the kerb lamp. He knew the street from the evening news feed. In fact, despite the passing of hours he could recall every minute detail. It was an unremarkable feat amongst his own kind, but here, negotiating contracts in a foreign system, it gave him a distinct advantage. At times like this, his memory was a burden as well. Stranded in the backstreets of Freeport, the murder scene came to him clear and unbidden, gnawing at his resolve, threatening to tilt his judgment.

He leaned away from the entrance to the pod station and cast his eyes along the street. It lay still and desolate now. On one side, a row of disused buildings hunched miserably in the drizzle, and behind them, barely visible against the night sky, rose the twisted lattice of the old skytram. On the other side there was an open lot, two burned-out transports standing sentry over a jumble of building debris. And there, in front of them, where earlier there had been a knot of professional activity, the pavement still wore its jade sheen.

It was the third shooting in this part of the city in the few days since D'Vani had docked. There were more dangerous places to do business, of course, systems where the rule of law was faint and distant, but even here in the Commonwealth's great capital he kept to the recommended routes, proceeding with all the caution of a seasoned traveller. Nevertheless, here he was, exactly where he shouldn't have been, at the wrong station for the Ancona Hotel, the station door closed firmly behind him and declining instructions. He turned away from the street and requested entrance again.

'Greengate is now closed,' the system said, crisply. 'My service re-commences at Mark 6.5. The nearest night station is Ancona. I have sent you route guidance and will be glad to continue your service there.'

D'Vani cursed under his breath and set out on foot, head bowed to the weather. Walking briskly, it wouldn't take long, but after a day of meetings in a foreign language, the mistake was more than frustrating. He fingered his cheekbone, bringing the route into his vision, a schematic of floating beacons to guide his way. The pod system advised him to stay on the main street, exposed to the elements rather than taking a more direct route under the tracks. He hesitated for a moment, the murder scene coming fresh to his mind, then took a set of steps down to an underpass, a damp and forbidding passage, soundless but for the ringing of his heels. Some reflex caused him to hunch his shoulders and draw his coat closer as he hurried towards a conveyor at the far end.

A shadowed figure emerged suddenly from a recess in the distance. It turned towards him as if waiting, and his heart responded with a sharp tug, adrenaline urging it to a faster rhythm. The figure adjusted the collar of its coat then took the conveyor up to the street. D'Vani exhaled, cleared his throat, then went on, chin held a little higher.

'Stop!' A voice echoed from a side-tunnel, bringing him to an abrupt halt. He spun around and peered into the shadows. It took a few moments for him to realise that the voice didn't belong to a person, but one of the feral animals from Freeport's Derelict Zone. A human. This one appeared particularly unthreatening. It was less than six units tall and draped in rags, with a mass of dark, filthy hair, and limbs that seemed fragile things compared with his own. Quite why wild creatures were tolerated on the streets of the capital he could never understand. It was a well-known Antarian indulgence, but he still found the idea of it shocking, even as a regular visitor to the system. He turned away, deciding not to respond.

'Stop!' The human said, again. 'Warm coat.'

'This coat is not for you, boy,' said D'Vani. 'Away you go, now. Off with you!'

The human was not deterred. It came out of the shadows, and now D'Vani could see it clearly. It was holding a pistol at his side. 'Gun!' it said. 'Coat - now!'

The muzzle of the weapon was shaking slightly, a row of amber lights showing it was still unprimed. D'Vani had never encountered a wild human before, and had certainly never heard of one attempting to use a pistol. The news feed pushed itself into his mind again. It was possible the human had seen the murder, picked up the discarded weapon, but still it seemed unlikely that the creature would understand how it operated.

'Coat now, shitface!' it said, and now it raised the gun level. D'Vani realised he needed to act quickly, to take back the initiative somehow. Whether they were domestic or industrial, the conditioned responses of humans were broadly the same on every world. They understood authority, respected strength and confidence. He took a step forward and raised his voice. 'Away with you! Do you hear me, boy? Away now!'

The human seemed to waver. Its voice became quieter, but its words were still unexpectedly bold. 'Coat now!' it said. 'Gun - you die!'

'D'Vani stamped his foot and shouted his command with the full force of his voice. 'Put that down!' he bellowed. 'Get away, I say! Go!'

The human retreated a step, its hand shaking as D'Vani started forward. Then it raised the pistol higher and closed one eye. The lights on the barrel went green. 'Die,' it whispered, and fired.

D'Vani hit the ground hard. The walls of the underpass reeled in his vision and the floor moved in waves beneath him. There was no trace of elemist on his coat, but he knew it was already doing its toxic work within him. He could feel it chilling his bowels, worming its blue strands under his skin, starting its relentless journey to his brain. The effect would be fatal unless he could get to a remedial post quickly, and even then, the odds were against him. He tried to raise a clinical patrol, but the elemist had entered his neural pathways, scrambling his communications. A stream of data came spinning across his vision, alerting him to his weakening vital signs. He tried to raise himself from the ground, to fight against the freezing tide, but the most he could manage was to prop his shoulder against the wall.

There was a shuffling sound to his right, and he turned, hoping to see another late-night traveller. It was the human again. It hadn't run off but stood watching from the shadows.

'It's…alright, boy,' said D'Vani. 'An accident. Just get help - please!'

The human stepped into the light and stared down at him, the gun still aimed. It glanced at the status display on the barrel, then lowered the weapon. 'I save,' it said. 'Stay here.'

D'Vani gasped as the elemist reached further into his organs. 'Save!' he said. 'Yes - good boy. Go for help! Quickly!'

The human shook its head slightly and crouched down, pointing to the power cell, bulging on the side of the weapon 'Save *gun*,' it said. 'Stay, see you die. Shitface.'

★

Emily's limbs refused to take instructions. She tried again to lift her head, but only managed to tilt her chin towards the edge of the mattress. There was nothing much to see. The cubicle was hardly any wider than her body, and there were no gaps or joints to break the sterile continuity of its walls and ceiling. A faint light provided a tinted glow to the enclosure, but revealed nothing to provide orientation, no clue to her location.

Emily's mind felt sluggish too. Not only were answers elusive, but it seemed that her brain couldn't even find the right questions. They were there somewhere, but just beyond the reach of rational thought. She closed her eyes again. She could feel her heart rate increasing, fear rising in her chest, pushing its way into her throat so that each breath came as an audible gasp.

How long the panic maintained its grip in that timeless space, she couldn't determine, but gradually her respiration seemed to settle, and she began to think again. She started with her senses. Her vision was working clearly, and she could hear her breath. There was a vague sense of fabric resting lightly on her skin, and from the corner of her eye she could glimpse a white sheet. The air felt warm and moist on her face, and it held a faint scent that she couldn't quite place. She began to think of things she knew, memories, things that were true and real. *The sea. The farm. The library in the town. No, that was long ago. I went away from Devon. A ship. Yes, I went to Africa. Then what?* She searched for something more, some event, anything that might provide a reference point. *Writing a letter. I sent a letter to Mr. Dunstone. Then, I got news of his passing. I heard in Africa – a telegram. I was with the children at Berseba. A scorching day. Someone came with a message. I left the class under the tree, with an exercise. Behind the building, reading the telegram in the cool of the stock cupboard. And then... something. A shape? A movement?*

'Hello! Help! Is anyone there? Hello!' *What's happened? Are you there, Mr. Dunstone? Have I died too?*

She tried to move again, but paralysis still held her from the neck down. Only her insides were capable of movement, nausea curling in her stomach, shifting under her diaphragm like a living thing. She turned her head and retched. First there was nothing, then she retched again and a mass of clear gel emerged from her mouth. It left her body slowly, reluctantly, then liquefied, trickling out of view.

A tone sounded softly above her head and she looked towards it. A point of light appeared and blinked at her, then the whole cubicle seemed to seize a breath, like someone released from the verge of suffocation. The point of light reached out across the cubicle to become a constant red line, fine at first, then stretching, widening. It hurt her eyes, but she couldn't look away.

Slowly the cell began to open, the roof lifting away and one of the walls dropping. Outside there was nothing but grey metal, a dimly lit corridor lined with compartments and marked at intervals with strange symbols. A sweet draught arrived from somewhere. Instinctively, Emily drew a breath, and then she was coughing more of the clear material. But there was some feeling coming to her limbs now, tingling, then cramping painfully, as if her blood was finding long-abandoned pathways through her tissue.

A low rumbling started beneath the floor, like a mill-wheel grinding dry grain, vibrations growing and spreading, as if the walls, the floor, the whole corridor was awakening. It was almost as if she was aboard one of the steamers at Southampton docks, trapped in its hold and casting-off from the Ocean Terminal. Emily reached out to push herself into a sitting position, but she was still too weak to exert any force. She shouted again, then listened as it echoed along the corridor.

'Help! Help me! Please!'

There were more sounds now, something hissing like a garden hose, the squealing of metal in long-awaited motion. Somewhere things were happening. For the first time, the thought occurred to Emily that there was danger in being found, and she was afraid. Things of dark imagining were coming, drawn by the sound of her voice. A scream rose within her and she clamped it tight between her teeth. Further down the corridor, doors were opening in succession. There were indistinct murmurings, footsteps.

*

Henik Varkesen shifted his position slowly, quietly, never taking his eyes from the activity in the plaza below his hide. He slid another layer of packing card between himself and the stone floor, his thoughts returning to the times when he had sat there more comfortably. Then, his balcony had looked across a vista of gleaming urban prosperity, the solus cast its gentle warmth on his guests, and the cocktails were always cold. In his memory, the guests were charming, eager to hear his stories of distant places and curious fauna, always keen to sponsor his next expedition to the desert planets of the Iota system.

If anyone had told him, ten years back, that Midsummer Plaza would become a wilderness itself, he would have considered it absurd. No one had seen hard times coming, or expected such a cruel toll. For the commercial zone, the decline had been catastrophic. At the plants, the docks, the warehouses, workers were no longer economic to keep. The androids were de-commissioned or placed in storage, but humans were just abandoned, left to fend for themselves. They turned feral, stripping the zone of anything that could be used, traded, or eaten, fighting to the death over a patchwork of territories that had once been business parks and shopping streets. Now, there was no need for a naturalist to travel interstellar, or even abroad. The behaviour of wild things could be observed within the city limits.

Henik adjusted his imager in anticipation of the coming drama. He had it focused on a tribe of ferals he called 'the Midsummer Clan'. They were searching the gutters of a conveyor opposite, sitting on each other's shoulders and passing down fallen fruit. The display of co-operation was unlikely to last for long. It would be disrupted at some point by some minor dispute, or perhaps the intrusion of a rival clan. On this occasion, it was the latter.

He had seen the scenario unfold before. A wild goat, or a scrub rodent would venture into the plaza, pursued by ferals from an adjacent territory. The males would rush forward shouting and hurling stones and would be met with a similar display from their rivals. Sometimes there would be injuries, but normally the interlopers would retreat, respecting the clan's possession of the square alone with its stark architecture and overgrown foliage troughs.

It was a boar that provided the flashpoint this time. A rare prize, it bolted from underneath the old skytram terminus pursued by a hunting party from the docks, racing to keep it from leaving their territory. Below the balcony, the Midsummer Clan reacted as Henik had come to expect, grabbing anything that might be used as a projectile and vocalising loudly in that harsh trilling tone unique to humans.

In the middle of the group stood the striking black-skinned female he had named 'Alka'. She stood at least six units high, and wore her overalls knotted at the pelvis. Her hair was drawn up into a wiry ridge that extended from her forehead right to the base of her skull. In one hand, she held a blue javelin and she gestured to her clan with the other, dispersing the males to the edges of the square alone. Now, as she advanced across the square, the boar took an unexpected turn and headed straight at her.

The animal lowered its head and charged, squealing its anger with every stride. Henik caught his breath and targeted his imager to capture the collision. Alka waited until the boar had closed to less than eighty units, then drew the javelin back until the tip rested against her cheek. She settled into a low stance, knees flexing and the sinews of her shoulder bulging in readiness. Still she waited, until just as Henik was sure she had left it too late, she snapped her arm forward and launched the javelin with a high-pitched shriek. It hit the boar square on the forehead and its legs crumpled mid-stride, the energy of its charge carrying it forward until it slid to a halt at her feet.

Alka wrenched the javelin from the animal's skull and squatted to examine it, seemingly unconcerned that the dockers were already sprinting across the square to claim the prize. She took no notice when the flanks of the Midsummer Clan rushed from under the porticos and fell upon them with alloy bats from the sports shop in the mall. It wasn't until the last moment that she seemed to hear the approaching footsteps and raised her head to see that one of the dockers hadn't been intercepted. He threw himself forward wide-eyed and she reacted instantly, thrusting the tail of the javelin into the dead boar and pulling the point down to meet him as he leapt. It took him cleanly through the throat and his body came to an abrupt halt as Alka held the javelin firm against his momentum. For a moment, he seemed to dance on his toes, mouth open, chin thrust to the sky. Then, slowly at first, he slipped forward, sliding down the javelin until his face rested on her fist.

The skirmish was over as quickly as it began. The enemy fled in disarray and the Midsummer Clan assembled around the boar, chattering excitedly. Alka pushed the docker's body from her javelin with her foot, then barked an instruction that had it dragged aside and arranged tidily. The clan members gathered around the boar and hoisted it onto shoulders, to be taken away to their encampment in the mall. They filed past Henik's balcony, some leaping and spinning, calling to each other in high-pitched voices, while others moved with solemn dignity, carrying the trophy in silence. Last in the line was Alka. She paused for a moment as if she had heard something, then returned to the docker's body and crouched to take something from his coat. She examined it as she walked away, pressing at its surface until a pattern of lights appeared. Henik knew what it was, and he got his hand to his own pod token just too late to shut it down. It emitted a bright tone, requesting a journey share, and triggered its own display, with Alka's location. Down in the plaza she walked with an easy grace, holding the token up in front of her and turning it over in her hand. Then as she passed below Henik's balcony, she lifted her head and stared up at his position.

*

Henik didn't move until the Midsummer Clan was out of sight. Then he crept from the balcony into his apartment, re-entering the civilised world with the closing of a door. There was little that remained there of his former life, though. The property was unsaleable and he had taken everything of value to his new home in the centre of Freeport. The apartment was little more than a shell now, but somehow, he couldn't bring himself to give up on it. In fact, with the subject of his studies close at hand, he often found he could work better at Midsummer than anywhere else. He tidied his notes on the battered dining table, wafting away the dust, then wandered from room to room, lingering in the doorways for no reason he could put into words. He went to the bathroom and relieved himself in the grating, wondering how he had ever been persuaded to cover the entire wall in mirror sheeting. His age was showing, though less in his body than his face, which was beginning to crease heavily along his cranial ridges and cheek bones. Not that it mattered, he thought; he had never been handsome in the first place, and his only interest these days was his work. It seemed a remote possibility that he would find someone to share his life now, someone who would understand him, tolerate his absences, someone who could endure views on human behaviour that were not always welcome in polite society.

In fact, Henik credited humans with even greater cognitive ability than he would admit publicly. The pod token was still a surprise, though. It was an attractive object he supposed, with its flashing lights and tones to provide amusement. Or perhaps Alka had taken it as a battle trophy. But grasping its purpose was quite another matter. *Did she hear my pass responding? Did she make a connection with the object in her hand, or was it just coincidence that she looked in this direction?*

A slight vibration started in his skull. He walked back to the balcony room and touched the side of his cheekbone. 'Henik,' he said simply, and slouched into an old chair in the corner. An ethereal figure materialised in front of him, the face recognisable, but the name eluding him until it appeared in yellow holographic characters.

'It's Yan Feyrsten here, Henik. I don't know whether you remember me. It's been a long time since National Service, so...'

'Yan! What a pleasant surprise. I'm sorry we didn't stay in contact. Whatever happened to you? I always wondered if you stayed in the service, went off to some desolate border outpost, perhaps. You were always the diligent one.'

'Well, for a while I did think I might stay in. But you know how it goes. Life just took a different turn. I haven't been off-world for years now. What about you? Your career seems unstoppable. I keep seeing you being interviewed, making statements. You're quite the celebrity, these days.'

'Not that - at least I hope not. It helps pay the bills, but it costs me in other ways. My work is all-consuming, so I am not always good company. And I am controversial in some quarters, as you probably know.'

'Well, we've had the worst economic slump in our lifetimes, Henik... and you're pressing for animal rights.'

'For humans. Only for humans.'

'Well, actually, it's a human I'm calling about. I think I've made a big mistake and I could really use some advice.' A rippling movement travelled along Yan's cranial ridges, betraying his discomfort.

'What sort of mistake?'

'I bought a human a few days ago, and it hasn't gone at all well. She's a real handful - not taking to her new environment. Resisting all the way.'

Henik sighed. 'Well, I've got to be honest with you - I really don't approve of the buying and selling of humans. I know that puts me out on a limb, but there you are. I don't think I'll be able help you.'

'Please, Henik, I don't know what to do! She's not eating and she won't respond to instructions. I've gone by the book, but it's no use. I was thinking about trying to take her back to the warehouse, but then I saw you interviewed on the news last night so...'

'What do you mean 'by the book'? What book?' Henik had a good idea what the answer would be. He would have bet his honour on it.

'Well, *The Human Handbook* seemed to be the best,' said Yan. 'It's the one everyone seems to use, anyway.'

'Sig Norvik. You're reading Sig Norvik. Look, he's great at the promotional stuff, I'll give him that, but as a serious anthrozoologist, I've got no common ground with him. Please don't tell me you've adopted his 'Assured Consequence' methodology.'

'Well...' Yan studied the floor, and his image lost some of its sharpness.

'You have, haven't you?'

'It seemed to make sense. I wasn't getting her compliance.'

'So, you hit her.'

'Well, discipline...yes.'

'Marvellous. Yan, you're an old friend, but I really don't know what to say to you. I study humans in wild settings. It really isn't my thing to work with pets. I object to it as a matter of principle and frankly, I don't find them very interesting when they've been bred for domestic captivity.'

'But that's just it. She is wild. She's just arrived on a transport.'

'What? From where? That could be really dangerous. You can't just go buying a feral, Yan. There are laws against it for good reason - you could be spreading industrial bio-toxins.'

'But she's not a feral! The transport came from Earth.'

'Earth? Who told you that? Believe me - she hasn't come from Earth. The war in that quadrant cut off the trade generations ago.'

'It was an old transport. It was picked up interstellar, shot full of holes. The cargo was mainly minerals, but there were a few humans as well. She was the only one still alive.'

Henik stared at the hologram, his mouth suddenly dry as his mind raced through the implications. *He has no idea, not the slightest understanding of what he's just said.*

'Henik? Will you help? Please, I really need you. I do think you would find her interesting.'

'Interesting? Yan, let's get this straight…you're seriously telling me that you've got a *natural?*'

'Well, yes, if that's the term. Very natural I would say. Is that bad?'

'It would be about as far from bad as you could possibly get. I doubt very much that you're right - but if you are, if they've really told you the truth, then you've got the only natural we've had on Antaris for generations!'

'Then you'll come?'

'I'm on my way. In the meantime, you better lock your doors.'

'Awakening' is the first chapter of The Callista Alignment, a completed science-fiction novel:

When Yan Feyrsten buys a new human to ease his loneliness, he has no idea how much trouble she will bring. Picked up on a drifting interstellar transport, Kali is something that hasn't been seen on Antaris in living memory – she's an Earth-born 'natural'.

Kali is the change Yan needs. Refusing to recognize herself as a mere animal, she is soon turning his life upside down. But with society in turmoil, Antarians must make hard choices about the humans in their midst. As a political crisis threatens to tear Yan and Kali apart, revolution awaits its cosmic signal, its moment of destiny – its leader.

The Interseers

Susannah Heffernan

(A novel extract)

Chapter 1

The ghosts of the angry dead are watching her. Beatrice stands at the mouth of the escalator above the pit of Canary Wharf station, looking up at tall office blocks. They are like stone pillars reverencing the God of Money. Beatrice is going home. It is dark now, but unsilent. Out of the corners, between the interstices they raise themselves. They walk in the beauty of this electric night. The murdered, the suicides, the long dead diseased from East London's dirty past. Sailors, fallen drunk into the docks and drowned. The starved poor. The mobsters, the slavers and their human cargo. The nameless, the cursed, the whistleblowers, the patsies whose mouths were silenced. Those who stood up and whose legs were broken. The villainous, the innocent. The slum dwellers. All here, unseen.

Beatrice glides through them, oblivious that her flesh and blood is cutting straight past their ethereality; hundreds of them, hanging in the air or walking up the escalator, impossibly.

Beatrice is on her way home from her new job. It's only a temp job, while she sorts her head out. From the print room to the front desk, she's delivered documents, done 'admin'. She's managed to see quite a lot of the bank, from the marble hall to the airless back office full of weary drones and their unwelcoming, hollow stares. She's glad to finish her shift, and get out of there. Thank goodness for the man in green overalls who lingered by the print room photocopiers, smiling. She acknowledged him a few times through the day. He was the only welcoming presence.

Quietly, she steps off the escalator, walking across the polished ticket hall, her contactless card sweeping her through the barriers into the station's deeper chambers. The second escalator is busier, the suits behind and in front of her jostling for position, as if the next train isn't just a couple of minutes away. 'Your heart attack,' she muses, standing still while the bankers run down the last few steps to make it onto a train ahead of her. A deliberate exhale, slow and deep, reminds her she has no need for their speed. She hears the rumble of a new train coming. And a sigh. Not hers. And another. She turns. The platform has emptied, only she is standing now, waiting for this train. Doors open. She gets on. Sits down. There's the sigh again. And again. Someone is breathing down her neck. And now she sees them. All around her. The dead.

His smile moves right in, up in front of her face. It's that man in green overalls. She acknowledges him. She thinks he's real. Why wouldn't she? Warm eyes, heavy-set, skin weathered, lined, kind. And a series of pictures flash before her, and all around her, and they engulf her until she's in the scene. The same man is driving a crane, and they are outside now, on a building site. He's expertly manoeuvring the huge machine, moving vast blocks of concrete between the iron strutted innards of some half-built tower block. The crane turns effortlessly for a few seconds, until it stops suddenly. Her eye zooms in on the top part of its long arm, to see it start to collapse, beginning to come apart, crashing down on the tiny cab and crushing the green-clad driver, burying him in red steel and grim, grey rubble.

She's lifted out of the scene, and his arms are around her firmly now. She's back in the tube train, looking into his tear-brimmed eyes. And now another hand grips hers, and a pale, terrified man is staring at her. She's back outside with him, high up on the roof of the JP Morgan building in the wind. It's freezing. His suit is flapping wildly. It's the light of the early morning and he jumps off the edge of the building. She plunges with him, hears his final scream as he hits the terrace of the ninth floor, breaking all his limbs, shattering his skull; he is drenched in blood and rain. His body is the focus of fascinated horror from the overlooking windows.

And all their arms are tightly round her now, as she recoils. The tube train heaves left and right. No more! No. They don't show her any more. They'll spare her for now. Because Beatrice is going to have to get used to it: to seeing all of it. She's an Interseer, and her channel is newly open. Their channel. To the world of those still living.

＊

Pretty soon it was April, and the job in Canary Wharf, with its long hours, had deadened her resolve to get out more. Beatrice could count her active friendships on the fingers of one hand. Still, she'd met someone, in a club about a week ago, and she'd been asked for her number. So maybe there was hope on the romantic front after all.

Walking past the flower shop on the South Colonnade, the enormous palms in pots, the garlands, wreaths and white lilies drew her in. Was it too clichéd to turn up to a first date with another woman bearing blooms? She summoned her sense of gallantry and dismissed her doubts, having spied a lilac display at the back of the shop. The pinks, the rich deep purples and their scents of subdued sensuality appealed to her. She grabbed a bunch, paid and headed back out into the chill air, the damp stems leaking a few drops of water onto her jeans. The speed of her thoughts and feelings blurred any true sense of time now, and she was at Waterloo. Coming up to the station exit was like coming up for air. Her life was coming up for air, perhaps.

Allegra was sitting in the soft light of the early evening, on the steps by the statue of Nelson Mandela. She glanced up to see Beatrice and gave her a delightful smile, beautiful, bright and open. She looked happy, in a way Beatrice had forgotten to be recently. A little flash of light had flared inside Beatrice and then was gone. Blue eyes, vivid blue, and cheeks that were round and soft and fresh. The face of an angel. Beatrice laughed out loud at herself at the thought. Allegra pulled Beatrice in for the briefest of hugs, the sweet lilacs pressed between them, and then she released her and fixed her with a laugh.

'Let me show you something,' Allegra said, and she leapt up the remaining steps. Beatrice followed and quickly they walked to the Tate Modern and into a side gallery, Allegra showing her staff pass. 'Do you like modern art?'

Beatrice did, and she was happy to be compliant as her new acquaintance led her through the small exhibition of futurist paintings full of mad colours, slewed figures slanting across canvases, geometric shapes twisting out of joint. They were mesmerising.

Then one painting, red with ochre brushstroke figures, and a sky of yellow and blue, mathematical but energising, caught her attention. It felt like the figures in it were moving, whirling in circular chaos. This one painting made her stand still and look.

'The Funeral of the Anarchist Galli. It looks like Hell,' Beatrice said. 'I'm not sure I like it, but it really grabs you, doesn't it?'

'I love it! I love all of them. I wanted to show you. I hope you don't mind?' Allegra looked at her, earnestly. When they had done the circuit of the small gallery, and emerged again onto the dusky Southbank, Beatrice looked out over the water, and the buildings, incongruously ancient and new, and she felt the ground beneath her shift slightly, so that she had to catch herself, and the Cheesegrater and Walkie Talkie and Shard appeared to lean to one side and bend for a split second, like a wave in the fabric of the sky. And then the image righted itself, and she was fine. She was really fine, she assured herself.

'Shall we have a drink?' Beatrice suggested, and Allegra was quick off the mark. 'Yeah. There's a nice place I sometimes go after work.' They crossed the Borough Market to a cosy wine cellar, finding a spot at the back of the bar where they could finally get acquainted. The questions and the wine flowed and were replenished, and Allegra told Beatrice about her art project and her little studio in New Cross. It turned out they lived about a mile apart, and they laughed about that, and Beatrice found herself doing that thing where you wonder if it's all a bit too good to be true, because everything feels like it fits. And she felt nervous and self-conscious for the first time, but intrigued, as she watched the curve of Allegra's full, neat lips, and ran her eyes over the honey strands of her hair untidily tied back to expose the exquisite chiselled lines of her jaw. The bones of her clavicle were just visible at the neck of her rather sensible jumper. Perhaps not date wear, but she got the feeling Allegra had no time for such pretences.

'So, you're a writer? What are your stories about?'

Full marks for remembering that from last weekend, Beatrice thought, and cringed slightly, recalling how, in the bravado fuelled by Pornstar Martinis, she hadn't mentioned her mundane day job. 'Well, I'm not actually writing very much right now,' she admitted. 'I've started a novel about a guy who dreams himself through all the colours of the rainbow, but to be honest, it isn't going anywhere. I'm a bit stuck.' She'd been 'stuck' for about three years. 'I write fantasy, about different worlds, that kind of thing. How people can, sort of, have worlds within them.'

Allegra looked totally interested. Beatrice wasn't sure if this was genuine, or just a talent she had.

'I like that. Worlds inside you. I suppose we've all got stuff inside; a bit like we're standing on a train platform going somewhere, carrying our emotional suitcase.'

Another little flare went off inside Beatrice. She felt Allegra's knees touch hers under the table. 'On the train platform? Waiting for a train to take us and our emotional baggage to the next station?' They both laughed, and Beatrice thought it hadn't taken them long to get so deep.

'I guess so, I mean, we've all got things we carry with us. You're very guarded, I think, aren't you Beatrice.'

Beatrice laughed a little uncomfortably at that. 'I don't know really.'

Allegra reminded her of a gamine Julia Roberts. She hoped she was older than she looked. About twenty-four? There was maybe five years between them, she estimated.

'Hurry up please. Chucking out time!' The blokey shout accompanied the brief clang of a bar-top bell, and all too soon they were stepping out into the dark night air. They had walked perhaps five steps when Allegra stopped and turned left, slipping into a quiet little side street. Beatrice followed, and her companion was facing her, close. The move was unexpected, but welcome, and her guard went down. She felt her shoulders encircled, and she wrapped her arms round Allegra's slim waist. She could feel Allegra's heart beating. Her own felt like it was pounding in her belly, and in her throat, and in the tips of her fingers as they stroked the knots of Allegra's narrow back. She breathed in the scent of violets from her as they pulled each other close, Allegra's lips, and then her tongue pressing against hers.

And when they released each other, they were silent for several slow seconds. 'I have to go.' Allegra whispered, and she drew her hand away; she was walking away, waving, then turning and sprinting off towards the station.

Beatrice stood still a while. Then she walked, alone, back to Waterloo.

On the tube, a woman wearing a Black Lives Matter t-shirt sat down opposite her.

And another, younger, solid-set woman, her hair braided and wearing a crumpled, but flouncy, petticoat dress with rolled up sleeves and smart heeled shoes with large buckles sat down in the seat beside her, sticking her elbows into Beatrice, and muttering something to herself. 'So, black lives matter, do they?' Her voice was harsh. Beatrice shuddered, as she was shaken from her post-date haze. She cursed the woman's bolshiness, as she continued in a loud American accent, leaning in a little too close for her liking. 'My life. What about my life? My life never mattered.' She looked like she would erupt... Beatrice looked around the carriage, seeking non-verbal reassurance from the other passengers that, yes, this person was mad, or at least an eccentric Shoreditchy type with great fashion sense but no social boundaries. No one met Beatrice's gaze. Heads down, fingering phones, or staring in front of them, in stubborn London Underground avoidance mode, where people exist in parallel, sensibly ignoring each other. She should move seats, but she didn't want to offend this woman, who appeared to be deeply troubled.

The train stopped. Some people got off, including the Black Lives Matter fan. The American woman stayed in her seat. Beatrice sighed. Only four more stops until she could get away from the awkwardness. A teenager and his giggling mate, tottered onto the carriage, just as the doors were closing, and he lowered himself into the occupied seat beside Beatrice. She involuntarily raised her arm to push the guy back, to alert him and save the woman from being sat on. He shot a sharp look at her, 'Woah, okay, okay,' and halted, just as his whole leg, back and arm were lowered into the seat, his body overlaying and merging into the space where the woman was already sitting. She sat back and let his shape coexist in the same frame as hers for an instant, before he rattily moved over to an opposite seat, glaring at Beatrice as if it were she who was mad.

The woman finally smiled, seeing Beatrice's shocked face, and chuckled. She laughed for a few seconds before she stared hard at Beatrice. 'Don't talk to me, darlin', if you can't bear being looked at like that. But listen. I want you to know what happened to me. Can you give me a little bit of your time?'

And Beatrice understood now. Her stomach fell. She thought back to her weird experience on the train at Canary Wharf. She'd wanted to tell people but hadn't. She couldn't understand it, so she'd shut it out. The wine she'd just drunk helped her to settle a little, as the woman froze the moment, literally froze it so it was no more than a picture, and only she and Beatrice were moving against a static background. 'My name is Ada, and I want you to help me. I want you to tell people about me. Do you think you can speak up for me?'

Ada reached out her hand toward Beatrice. The skin was deeply cracked and lined, and on the palm a seared red scar, a letter 'M'. Her hand rested on Beatrice's shoulder as she spoke:

'I was born in the place your kin would know as Nigeria, in Essaka, in the Igbo province. My name means firstborn, and I grew up with my brother, Olaudah and my sisters. When I was thirteen, they took us away.' Ada's voice trembled despite its strong, deep tone, as she recounted how she was kidnapped by a gang of men and women, how she was beaten and imprisoned in a stinking stone cell for a week, and how she was thrown on board a ship bound for America.

All around her, on the static train carriage, Beatrice was now bombarded by very loud voices, shouts and screams, and the thwack of fists on bones and Ada was crying now as she spoke, and Beatrice was panicked, looking around her. The passengers were still a frozen backdrop, and the shouting wasn't in English. She grabbed onto Ada, who felt solid and real. 'Come with me,' Ada said, over and over, 'Come with me, come with me.'

And they were walking together now, through the carriage. Ada held her, as Beatrice shielded her head with her hands and yelled. But there was no impact and the train wall felt buttery wet as she was pulled through it, and now she was running down the dark tunnel with Ada, dodging the tracks. Tripping on the huge iron connectors, feeling a sharp stab as her ankle twisted under her. But they didn't stop. It was freezing all of a sudden, and the attack sounds became the sounds of a woman quietly moaning. It was Ada.

No it wasn't. Ada was here, holding her, not crying any more, pushing her on, down the tunnel. But what looked like the face of Ada rushed into close-up view in front of her, as a projection on the tunnel wall, and then it showed her naked, lying on the wet wooden deck of a ship, and over her a tall red-headed man. Hitting her, hitting her, again and again, then a quick snarl and snap of his whip as he lashed her across the breasts. She was tiny. He was so huge. She screamed out, and Beatrice screamed as well, and shut her eyes. And the images and the sounds were still playing out on the wall. She couldn't shut them out.

The flesh and blood Ada had stopped running, not letting go of Beatrice. 'Don't close your eyes. Please, Beatrice, open your eyes. You have to see.'

And Beatrice watched the younger Ada's flogged body get thrown below deck, as if a sort of camera was following in close-up down the crowded hole where too many huddled and sweating women's bodies crouched, or lay unconscious, or gulped water from metal cups. Some were laughing, others were shouting, some were dazedly staring straight ahead with dead eyes. Water splashed Ada's chest, thrown in desperation to keep her living. And the 'camera' stayed fixed on her blood-flecked face as she recoiled.

'I lived. It would have been better I'd died that day. At least I'd have been spared sooner. I'd tried to jump overboard, believe me, I tried, so many times.'

'Stop this. Please, Ada, make it stop!' Beatrice felt everything pounding, and she was breathing too hard. Dread, a huge, horrible dizzy dread. She wanted out. The dark of the tunnel, now the projection had stopped, was broken by only the low glow of the side lights, and the darkness was soupy and thick and was grasping her, and she felt she was falling into it. Ada. Ada felt real. But she could not be real. This was a horrid rehash of stuff she'd read, and films she'd seen about slavery. This was a mad dream. Was it a lucid dream?

The Black Lives Matter woman earlier. That was it.

'Yes, that's it,' Ada said quietly. 'That's exactly it. You think that woman sat by you by accident earlier?'

'What do you mean?' Beatrice was rattily shouting now. 'I don't want this. Get out of my head!'

'You think I'm in your head?'

'Fuck off. Fuck off. I don't want this!'

And the picture of Ada came back onto the tunnel wall. This time, she was standing next to a smartly dressed, much older man, his hair up in a ponytail, in breeches and velvet jacket; and two women, one older, one younger than Ada. The younger one naked, the other about twenty, wearing a simple shift dress, all arm in arm.

'This is my kin. We're all united in death, Beatrice,' Ada said calmly, standing beside her. 'Go home now.'

*

The day after, everything was numb.

Beatrice took the day off work. It was grey and cold and relatively silent in the very early morning as she left her flat. She lived on the seventh floor, overlooking the DLR and the view of it snaking around the bend into Deptford Bridge station was one she'd always liked – it was also the reason she was paying over the odds to live in a tiny glass box above a shitty South London street. But this morning, Beatrice wanted nothing to do with trains. Or buses, or cars, or even people.

She'd felt she had to get up and get out. And walk. She grabbed an Americano from the corner of Greenwich High Road and set off. But not to work. Cutting by the side of building sites, she ended up on Creek Road, walking without thinking, putting one foot in front of the other, wrapped in her hoodie and jacket until she got to Greenwich itself. She'd passed the new Waitrose, its lights glimly suggesting life half-awake, and nodded to a couple of early morning workers, off to clean offices or paint on construction sites. She slipped down the side of some flats to reach the riverfront, and stood watching the gulls swoop down to peck at rubbish at the water's edge, and the green-grey stretched out towards the Shard and the strange Westminster skyline in the distance.

There was a text from Allegra she hadn't read yet. It had been sent close to midnight. There had been no space in her head for it last night. All the lust, the excitement at meeting someone new, their overly intimate chat, that kiss. It felt flat now. And the horrible feeling of dread was there again in her stomach, in the small of her back. The woman, Ada. She thought of her. Beatrice clung to the railings and stared at the lapping water creeping up the muddy bank and falling back, and she tried to breathe in the fresh air, listening to the birds loudly chattering, and watched a small boat motoring past. The breeze blew through her.

The text said, 'You're lovely. Thanks for tonite.'

Nothing more. Oh, okay. It was lovely. She was lovely. Lovely Allegra. But Beatrice felt like she had a hangover despite not drinking all that much really, and she felt the loveliness was a little thin next to whatever the fuck had happened on that train. She covered her face with her hands and rested her head on the railing, leaning against it and listened. Listened to the birds, and the wind, and tried to lose herself in the moment, feeling she was a mad girl at the edge of the world.

A Call from London

Beth L. Thompson

(A novel extract)

Chapter 1

The bus was halfway down Mount Pleasant when Johnny, fluffy-headed and spring-heeled, watched it sink into the hill. The ground should instead have opened up to reveal one fat middle finger. He would just tell them that the bus driver was a twat. Again. He zipped up his leather jacket, took a drag of his cigarette, swaggered into town.

Walking down Mount Pleasant always means that, at some point, you will find yourself thrust neatly between the lofty gazes of Liverpool's two adjacent cathedrals, as Johnny did on his early-morning slogs to the practice rooms. Liverpool Metropolitan Cathedral, or Paddy's Wigwam, looks down from Mount Pleasant. Liverpool Cathedral though, the Anglican, looks down on the city from St James Mount, or Mount Zion as some like to call it. The pair lock eyes somewhere in the middle of Hope Street.

Stand in the right spot and you will find the money shot – a framed painting in a grandma's kitchen. Johnny had always found it funny that they were placed like that, spiritual and physical opponents. It was as if they were two boxers, the city their ring. Same fight, different songs for the crowd.

As he approached Lime Street, Johnny sucked on the last dregs of his cigarette, watched its final breath stretch out before him in one long, grey tendril. He flicked the stump onto the steps of the station where it was joined by hundreds of others, most of them lipstick-stained. Johnny thought Liverpool at seven a.m. was the purest thing. It was raw and undiluted. It was the most beautiful woman in the world waking, curling her toes. It was a red stiletto wedged in a grid without a story.

The clouds were streaked and grey, seagulls circling and mewing. He wondered if they were singing. Ship horns could be heard at the docks, exhaling in deep moans, drawing up their anchors. Those two silhouettes, the guardians of the city, could be seen over Queen Square, standing tall between Johnny and the river. It was as if one set of wings was not enough for Liverpool, as if those Liver Birds were stuck, perched eternally contemplating flight to remind the city to fly because they cannot.

Johnny put on his headphones and continued to walk towards Dale Street, Norwegian Wood playing.

*

The lads had been in the rehearsal room for an hour before Johnny showed up.

'Our kid needs to get a grip and grow up,' Jay spat. 'We could get a call from London any day now. We need to sound as tight as we are on the EP but all soft lad cares about is how tight his fuckin' jeans are.'

'Alright, lad. He'll be here soon. You know what he's like,' Billy said.

'Yeah, I know him better than you do, Bill. Don't be makin' excuses for him. We're relyin' on him and he fuckin' knows it.'

The door swung open on its rusted hinges, making an uncomfortable squeaking sound as Johnny entered. 'You chattin' shit about me again, Bro?'

Billy and Sean welcomed Johnny with a harmonic, 'Alright, lad,' and continued adjusting their instruments.

The building was run-down and the room was dusty. But it was a place to practise, for now. There were talks about turning the place into flats. Billy, the drummer, had his kit set up against the wall. The others dotted around him, their cables streaming like umbilical cords, connecting them to speakers.

'What was it this time, ay? Did you have to stop and write in your diary on the way? Or have you crawled from some bird's house again?' Jay probed.

'Bus driver's a twat,' Johnny uttered, sitting down on the floor and taking a book from the back pocket of his jeans: *The Lords and the New Creatures: Poems by Jim Morrison*. With a small pencil, he underlined the words, "In the womb we are blind cave fish."

'Get the fuck up, John. You've wasted enough of the band's time.'

'Have I, yeah?' Johnny remained on the ground, staring up through his long hair and into his brother's face.

There were only three years between them. Johnny, the youngest, was eighteen and Jay was twenty-one. Jay's hands were made for building like his dad's. But they could *really* play guitar. The lads found it curious to watch someone so rough around the edges produce softness the way he did with his guitar. It was like watching a bear produce a fine watercolour.

Jay turned his back on Johnny and began fumbling his heavy fingers around jacks and cables.

'I've been writin' some new stuff that I want you all to have a look at,' Johnny said.

'We haven't got time for your fuckin' poetry now, John,' Jay said.

'Yeah? If it wasn't for my writin', you wouldn't have anythin' to fuckin' play, would you?'

'Right, lads. Come on. We've got to run through the full set – really polish it,' Billy cut in.

Billy had gone to school with Johnny and was his best friend. Sean worked in construction with Jay and slapped bass like his life depended on it. As far as he was concerned, it did. The band were influenced by rock 'n' roll, had *something*, were going *somewhere*. They hired the rehearsal space twice a week and their music could be heard from the street outside, riffs and licks scurrying through drainpipes with the rats.

Johnny got up, slipped off his jacket, positioned himself behind the mic. He looked into the microphone in the same way that he eyed the girls on Seel Street. All show, masking deeper disinterest.

*

Jay and his girlfriend, Abbie, had been together for three years. They both still lived at home and were trying to save up enough money to get a place together. They had both scraped by in school but Jay was hardworking now. Even if his heart wasn't in it. Abbie had had some success with her hairdressing business but only just earned enough to get by. Most weekends, they stayed together at either Abbie's mum's house, or the O'Connor house.

It was the Saturday after the lads had sent their EP to one of the biggest record labels in London.

'Do you think you'll hear back, Jay?' Abbie asked, stroking the nape of his neck as they sat on his bed.

'I can only hope so, Ab.'

'I think you will, you know. You've got the sound, the look—'

'Have we, though?'

'Stop it, Jay. You know you've got talent.'

'Have I, though? I just know music's all I fuckin' have. It's the only thing I've ever been okay at. I just don't like anythin' else. I can't do anythin' else.'

'Lies. You've got music and you've got me,' Abbie told him.

Jay's lips gave way to a half-smile before his features hardened again, 'I don't want to be stuck doin' the same job for the rest of my life. I need this.'

'Just keep tryin', Jay.'

*

A nightclub in Liverpool. Even the walls sweated on Saturday nights, windows steamed and the glue beneath fake eyelashes faltered. Booth dwellers baptised themselves in buckets of vodka, while the Rockys and Adrians stood at the bar. The indie kids could be found outside in the beer garden, exchanging cigarettes and winks, their legs dangling from the fire escape. Drunk girls made promises to each other in toilets before disappearing into the city like forgotten dreams. Saturdays were the same old song but everybody's favourite.

Johnny and his sister, Élodie, went out together most weekends. Élodie was the middle child, nineteen-years-old, had dark hair like Johnny's that fell in curls. Along with Jay, they made up the O'Connor clan. The children of Mary and Frank O'Connor – O'Connor, from the Gaelic Ó Conchobhair, originally Cú Chobhair, meaning, "hound of desire".

Johnny knew that if he wanted a drink any time soon, he'd have to send his sister. 'Go on, Él, they'll serve you quicker. They won't serve me till I've got tits.'

'Alright, what do you want?' she asked with a wide smile. She wore red lipstick and stood erect on tall skinny legs, identical to Johnny's.

Johnny wore a paisley shirt, half-buttoned, adorned with his mother's rosary beads. Saturday nights were about what you wore.

Once they were served, Johnny and his sister took their drinks to a bench outside where they could smoke.

'So, how's the band?' Élodie asked, lighting her cigarette.

'Alright, yeah…' Johnny took the lighter from Élodie's hand and lit his cigarette.

'Still not heard back about the EP?'

'Still waitin'. I'm not too bothered, like.'

'Our Jay is though, isn't he? He won't stop talkin' about it. He really wants this.'

'Yeah, he's doing my fuckin' head in. He needs to chill.'

'But what if you actually made it, though? You thought about that?'

'Don't know.'

'John, you're talented. Jay is too, like. But you, you could really go somewhere. Don't fuckin' waste that,' Élodie exhaled, smoke rolling in grey waves around them.

'What about you? You could be travellin' everywhere with your modellin'. But you're too scared to leave the city.'

'I just don't know if it's time yet.'

'Well, when is?' Johnny asked, sipping his beer.

'I don't know. When's it time for you?'

'Fair enough,' Johnny said and the pair laughed, sharing a brief silence in the bustle of the beer garden.

'Johnny, lad!' called a voice from within the pulse of things.

'Léo!' Johnny beamed at the sight of his flatmate approaching from across the garden. Léo was one of three lads Johnny was living with in his new student house on Smithdown Road. Léo was French and had gained a scouse twang since arriving in Liverpool to study.

'Want a drink, lad?' Léo howled over the club's music, before being hauled back into the riptide of the crowd, perfumed bodies engulfing him.

Since the band had been doing well and he had started university, Johnny had acquired quite a social circle.

'We'll see if we can catch him up later,' Johnny said.

'Uni's going well then, yeah?' Élodie asked her brother, 'I miss you in the house.'

'Yeah, it's good. It's different.'

'You're clever like Dad. You always have been.'

'Shut up, you. Anyway, is our Jay goin' to replace me as your best mate?' Johnny winked, the pair stubbed their cigarettes in the ashtray and headed back into the club.

Having danced away the hours, Johnny and his sister walked back through town, arms linked and shivering as the night turned into morning. The sky was powder blue and littered with pink streaks. Liverpool's buskers decorated street corners, looked down at the copper in their hats, fantasised about playing stadiums. Drunk crowds gathered around them, singing out of tune. Others looked down at their vomit, soiling the steps of the Bombed-Out Church. Elsewhere, a woman hobbled barefoot across the cobbles, next to a man shaking his head. The pigeons, at this hour, were more hopeful than anybody, discovering and devouring polystyrene trays of half-eaten chips before seagulls had the chance to ransack them.

The closer to Lime Street you were, the better chance you had of getting a taxi. Seeing the sacred yellow light of a black taxi on a Saturday night was like being in a sinkhole and spotting a ladder. Forty minutes and a trip to The Lobster Pot later, Johnny and Élodie were in a taxi home. Lately, after nights out with his sister, Johnny had been making a habit of staying over at the family house in West Derby.

Once they were home, they tried their best not to wake Jay or their parents, hushing and laughing their way through the door and into the shadows of the house.

'Night, John,' Élodie whispered, before wobbling slowly upstairs, heels in her hands.

'Night, Él,' Johnny said and walked into the kitchen to get a glass of water.

Slumped and asleep on the kitchen table was Frank. An empty bottle of whiskey lying next to him. Johnny paused in the doorway, watched him for a slow minute. Nothing much had changed since he'd left. In the half-darkness, he filled a glass with water, knowing his dad wouldn't hear a thing.

Frank's family were the descendants of Irish who had moved to Liverpool in the nineteenth century. After struggling to find jobs, it was impossible for them to afford fares to the U.S. and so they made a life in Liverpool. Frank was born and raised in Liverpool, worked building ships until losing his job in the eighties and becoming depressed soon after.

Anyone that knew him would tell you that he was one of those rare kinds of men – a book in one hand and a glove in the other. Frank's darkness was so much a part of his genius that it became him in the way that nightfall presents to us a new world. Johnny knew the truth. Not that they ever spoke too deeply about it. They'd always had a sort of silent understanding of each other. He knew that his dad's mind had forever been as restless as the waves beneath the ships he built. When Frank spoke about his past, about his days working on the docks, it was as if those ships were the things that kept him above the deep all those years. As if every bone in his hands had willed stability as he worked.

On his way out of the kitchen, Johnny paused once more, the birds beginning to sing with the dawn. 'Night, Dad.'

Johnny lay in his old bed that night, soaked in a familiarity that was not so familiar any more. His old dusty light that had looked down on him for years was changed in some way. And outside was the same tree, swaying to the same old rhythm. But the sight of it now, produced a different feeling.

Chapter 2

Frank and Mary met when they were just fifteen. They simply met and they simply knew. Mary would get the same bus to school as Frank every morning and stare intently into his face. He looked remarkably like Elvis, the love of her life. Frank stared back. In many ways, Mary was the perfect complement to Frank. She was tall but sylphlike, looked as if she would blow away with the wind if she were not careful. Her mind though, was iron, unwavering. She knew exactly what she wanted. After months of eyeing each other, Frank eventually plucked up the courage to ask: 'You got something wrong with your eyes, love?'

Mary made the best breakfasts on Sundays, especially when Johnny was home for the weekend. She was in the kitchen frying eggs, singing Love Me Tender, when the phone call came. Jay's phone buzzed from the table in the hallway, vibrating through the house.

Johnny scrambled at the sound, sprung from his bed and looked for the nearest item of clothing. The day marked one whole week since the band had submitted their EP. If they hadn't received a call within a week, they hadn't been successful.

Johnny appeared at the top of the stairs mouthing, 'Who is it?'

'Go away!' Jay ordered, approaching the phone and scanning its screen. An unknown number. 'Hello?'

'Jay, it's me, Abbie.'

'Oh, for fuck's sake, Ab...' Jay exhaled. His face had fallen at the hollow realisation that the band had now, quite possibly, been rejected by one of the biggest record labels in London. 'Whose phone are you callin' from—'

'Jay, listen...'

Sensing the tone in her voice, Jay fell back to earth and panicked. Abbie had gone back to her mum's house last night after feeling sick with a stomach bug. 'Are you alright, Abbie? What's up?'

'I'm at my mum's, I need you to come here.'

'Now? But I've—'

'Jay, I'm pregnant.'

Johnny dropped his feet, step-by-step, down the stairs. 'Jay? Jay, lad? What's happened?'

Mary had overheard Jay on the phone and came running through from the kitchen, her brown eyes electric. 'Everythin' alright, Son?'

Jay stood still, listening to the phone.

'Jay? Hello? Are you there?' Abbie's muffled voice was audible through the phone.

Jay stared at the floor and then at Johnny, 'Everything's over.'

Mary softened her voice, putting her hand on Jay's arm when she saw the expression on his face. 'Tell us what's happened, lad?'

'Will someone please tell me what the fuck is goin' on?' Johnny pleaded from the stairs. 'Is it the label?'

Élodie appeared next to her brother, the two of them peering wide-eyed over the banister.

Jay attempted to pull himself together, the news still ringing along with the tinnitus in his ears. 'It's Abbie. She's pregnant.'

They all stared at him, trying to read what he was feeling. Mary instantly put her arms around her son. 'It's goin' to be okay; I'm here for you. We *all* are. But listen, Son, you need to phone her back now, the poor thing. She's probably terrified.'

Élodie came down the stairs and hugged Jay. Johnny sat down on the stairs.

Jay approached him slowly, 'You happy, then? You won't have to play with me anymore. You can make it on your own. I won't be holdin' you back. It's over.'

'Stop it, Jay. Phone your girlfriend back.'

Mary and Élodie stood side by side against the wall, watching.

'The band would've got somewhere sooner if it wasn't for you and your fuckin' poetry – your fuckin' posin' around town. You're a selfish fuckin' twat!'

Johnny stood up, 'Hang on, how's everythin' my fault? You've blamed everythin' under the sun on me since I was fuckin' born. Get a grip, Jay! You're a big boy now. Stop blamin' me for your own shit. You think the whole world owes you a favour.'

'That's enough!' Mary broke in.

'Come on, John, leave him. He's just upset,' Élodie added.

The veins in Jay's temples were visible as he pressed his forehead against Johnny's, 'It's your fault the band hasn't done well. It's all your fuckin' fault…'

'Come on, then,' Johnny encouraged his brother, 'I'm not the fuckin' Yoko here, your girlfriend is.'

With that, Jay made a blow to Johnny's stomach, forcing him to fall backwards, winded on the stairs. Johnny tried to wrestle as Jay raised his arm, ready to swing for his face.

Frank appeared from the smoke of the kitchen, Mary's eggs burning. 'Get up, soft shites! I'm tryin' to read my fuckin' paper in peace here.'

'There's more important things goin' on out here than your paper, Frank,' Mary told him. 'Abbie's pregnant and Jay's too busy beatin' Johnny to phone the poor girl back. Where's the phone, Jay? I'll ring her.'

Jay stood up and cast his eyes to the floor.

'Jay, stop being selfish for a minute of your life and do what's right,' Frank said. 'Get in your car and go to Abbie. Nothing's over. You'll both be over if I see you actin' like that again.'

Johnny looked to the floor, his hand clutching his stomach.

'One day, Jay, you'll be old enough to realise how young you really are.' Frank's words rocked the house. The budgie stopped chirping in the living room and Jay left through the front door.

*

Johnny stuck around a while longer following the news. When the evening came, he sought out his dad to say goodbye. He found Frank in the kitchen at the table, where he'd sometimes sit to read, often to write and mostly to drink.

The orange glow at the tip of Frank's cigarette was bleeding through ash, illuminating the darkness of the kitchen. Lava piercing through the cracks of the atmosphere. Frank's skin was pale and weathered. His hair, still jet-black, had never been dyed. He lifted his eyes from his book, peered over his glasses at Johnny. He was reading *The Old Man and the Sea*. 'You off now, Son?'

'Yeah, Dad. Got some reading to do.'

'Listen, can you have a word with your sister before you leave?'

'Yeah, what for? What's happened now?'

'Nothing. Well, she's been signed in London. She found out last week but she wouldn't say anythin' to you because she's scared to leave home – to leave us. She's been cryin' to Mary. Mary's been cryin' to me.'

'Shit. That's… amazing. Yeah, I think she needs to go.'

'They can sort accommodation for her down there in a house with other models. I think it's the best thing for her. She could really get somewhere down there.'

'She could.'

'Everythin' that's happenin' with Jay now is probably goin' to make her want to stay even more.'

'Nah, I'll talk to her.'

'She thinks the world of you, lad. I know she'll listen to you.'

Nothing more was said but Johnny remained seated opposite his dad at the table. His eyes roamed out of the window, across the street and into nothingness. Into thought. Content in each other's company, they relished the silence.

'Don't be like me, Son.' Smoke swam from Frank's mouth and framed his face like a grey aura.

'What are you saying that for, Dad?'

'I mean, be better than me. Do everythin' you can. Don't be held back by your thoughts. Or by anybody else's fuckin' thoughts. Do what you want, while you can, lad. Just go for it.'

Johnny sat still for a moment, listening to the slow progress of the kettle coming to a boil. The blackness of the kitchen cradled both men.

'I love you, Dad.'

'I love you too, Son.' Frank cleared his throat to cough.

Mary appeared in the doorway, 'Did neither of you think to turn a bloody light on?'

*

Johnny and Élodie sat on the steps of the family home as it was turning dark.

'Dad's told me about London, Él.'

'Yeah?'

'You need—'

'I know what you're goin' to say: I need to go, follow my dreams. Try new things.'

'Yeah, well, you do.'

'I've already decided, John.'

'Yeah?'

'I'm goin'. I'm goin' to London.' Élodie choked on these words, her eyes beginning to water. Summer was ending and a cool breeze came with the night, giving her arms goose pimples.

Johnny put his arm around his sister and they stared ahead of them at the houses opposite. A gang of kids were playing football on the grass verge at the end of the road. 'You're goin' to have a new start – by far the most excitin' thing that's happened in this family.'

'Says you, Shakespeare.'

'Fuck off,' Johnny laughed, 'what made you change your mind anyway?'

'Jay.'

Johnny's face changed.

'He's wanted so much his whole life. One thing after another has faded away or got in his way. I can't do that, John. I can't stay.'

'I get it. You're right.'

'It'll kill me leavin' Mum. And Dad… and you.'

'What do you mean? I'm goin' to be stayin' over all the time, partyin' with you and your model mates.'

Élodie laughed, sending one rolling tear through her make up.

'Ay, you better not go all cockney! You're a Scouser; don't forget it.'

'Never.'

When it was time for Johnny to leave, he embraced his sister in the doorway, brother and sister communicating in their own silent telepathy. 'You're goin' to be fine, Él. This is life-changin'. We're goin' to look back at this. And I'm goin' to text you every day. I'll need someone to take the piss out of Jay with, won't I?' Johnny flashed a cheeky smile.

Élodie laughed a sad musical laugh. It was a song they hadn't heard before. Her stomach sank at the thought of Johnny leaving. Her brother walking down the steps of that house would be like a full stop.

'Love you, Él,' Johnny said, kissing his sister on the cheek before walking down the steps and onto the street.

Élodie swallowed as she watched her brother walk away. She wrapped her arms around herself and paused once more, looking at the street she'd known her entire life. It looked different now. The kids had been called in by their mothers after the streetlamps went out.

For the rest of the evening, she couldn't shake the image of those Liver Birds, stood solid and proud, from her mind. What good was Big Ben? She'd despise that cyclops. At least for a while, until she settled – because it didn't have wings. Leaving Liverpool was like losing a limb. Phantom pain she'd have to adapt to.

*

When Johnny arrived back at the student house, the lads were sat around the TV watching the match.

'Johnny, lad! Come and watch the game with us,' Leo called.

'Alright, Lee – I will in a min.' Johnny continued up the stairs and into his bedroom. He turned on the light, revealing the posters of Morrissey and Led Zeppelin lining the walls, the dreamcatcher hanging over his mattress. He lay flat on his bed, pulled a book from the bedside drawer: *Wilderness: The Lost Writings of Jim Morrison*. With a pencil, he traced the lines, "Now dance/or die sleek & fat in your/reeking seats, still/ buckled for flight."

Poetry

Beth L. Thompson

The Swimming

Throw me in the river; watch me float.
Arcane earthmark carried by the silt.
I will make a ladder of your rope.

I am the sweet dew-bead sweat of earth,
the ragged breath of a fallen crow.
Throw me in the river; watch me float.

Strip me against wood and discover
my breasts, shaped like your stones.
I will make a ladder of your rope.

Your men can tie my thumbs to my toes.
My girl, like some winged thing, will seep out.
Throw me in the river; watch me float.

Look at my pale skin, strung up above
the stream bed! I won't sink for you, no.
I will make a ladder of your rope.

And when my ash bleeds grey into air,
it will settle on moth wings, beating so,
throw me in the river; watch me float.
I will make a ladder of your rope.

Calling

After Li Bai

Crow, I hear you caw *caw*
from a near wall, yellow clouds
call your name and I swear

you call mine. Some darkness
intertwined in that gruff song
like the coarse hand

of an old lady spinning yarn
in the mist of her life. But
I am a river girl, green,

not yet part of that machine.
So why do I fly to you?
From wall to wall in my mind –

that lone room, that cage-tomb
where all the little black birds
fester and die.

Merry Christmas

Alexander Musleh

(A short story)

George relished the snow, which rarely graced the hills of Bethlehem. This year however, George's youthful hopes for a white Christmas were granted. He ate his warm rice pudding gleefully, the smell of cinnamon complementing the festive ambiance perfectly.

Uncle Basil's little pastry and cocktail shop in Nativity Street provided George with an unobstructed view of the church. Its plaza thronged with holiday worshippers, while festive shoppers trotted about from kiosk to kiosk, eager to get the most of this rare opportunity to hold a Christmas market. The Church of Nativity's snow-clad crosses shone brightly, reflecting the seasonal decorative lights. A gentle reminder that even during these turbulent times, some peace was still possible.

*

George recalled the events of the past few months, when the soldiers and the armed men stood off against each other at the church. For weeks, no one could go outside. His mother cried frequently, complaining that Jesus's birthplace was being defiled.

He didn't understand what was going on and why everyone was fighting. 'Intifada' his parents would say. He hadn't gone to school in over three months. The bad men with tanks were all around the city. They didn't let him play outside, sometimes for days.

Mom and Dad also complained about the rude resistance fighters, who liked to start shooting near people's houses.

Most nights, George could hear the loud bangs. Sometimes they would leave big holes in his windows and Dad had to fix them. He was used to it by now. If he heard the guns, he would run to his little sister Elisa's bedroom and hold her hands, guiding her towards the stairwell. Daddy was clever, an engineer. Daddy said that the stairwell was the safest place to be. Most of the week they slept there, hugging each other for warmth. George missed the comfort of his bed.

It wasn't all so bad though. When he could play with his friends they would go out scavenging for bullet casings. Most of them were crappy Kalashnikov bullets made in Egypt, the ones the resistance fighters used. Sometimes, they would find some of the good ones. Those were the ones that came from M16s and the bigger M60s. He had a few of those, all used of course. But that didn't matter, it still meant that he had one of the best collections. Now, however; he was the master of bullets, the whole gang would be jealous.

It was last week's events that had cemented his status, when Dad told him that he could go and play outside for a couple of hours. He was on his way back home after seeing his friend Jamal when George saw one of the big tanks. It was much bigger than he had imagined, far too large for Bethlehem's tiny streets. He ignored his mother's warnings about not getting too close to the soldiers and approached to get a better look.

Suddenly, the top hatch opened and a soldier ascended. His face was chiselled; a prominent scar was visible on his right cheek. George wanted to run, but fear got the better of him.

'What are you doing kid?' asked the soldier in broken Arabic. 'Go home, now! Curfew is almost over.'

'I'm…I'm just looking…Is that tank a Merkava?'

'Why, yes. Yes, it is,' said the soldier with a chuckle 'How do you know that?'

'I have one just like it, but smaller! Daddy bought it for me last Christmas from Israel.'

'Really? And what does your dad do?'

'He's an engineer, a good one, that's why he works in Israel.'

'What's his name?' asked the soldier, his lips twitching into a smile.

'Andrew.'

'Andrew. So, you're a Christian, huh? And what's your name?'

'George.'

'George. That's a good name. So tell me kid, what do you want for Christmas?'

George thought long and hard. Would this man really give him a Christmas present? He seemed to be nice, not as bad as Mom and Dad made the soldiers out to be. George remembered his bet with Jamal. If he could just get one, he would win Jamal's collection as well.

'Can I have one of your bullets?' said George.

'Come again? You want one of my bullets?'

'Yes!' said George.

The soldier looked confused, unable to make sense of George's unusual request.

'Why do you want one of my bullets?'

'I have a bet with my friend.'

The soldier looked around him. For a split second, George could see a concerned look on his face. It quickly disappeared though, morphing instead into a look of mischief, a slight smile.

'Come here,' said the soldier.

George approached, his mother's words a distant echo. He was going to get his Christmas present. The soldier unfastened a large ammunition clip from his belt. He extracted a bullet. It was a big one.

'Is that from a M60?' asked George.

'Yes,' replied the solider as he gently removed the bullet from its casing. He proceeded to extract the gunpowder and reassemble the bullet.

'Here you go kid. You can tell your friends this is a live one. That way maybe you can win your be...'

'Elan!' A sudden yell from within the tank. The rest of it was in Hebrew. George couldn't understand anything.

'Go on now, curfew is starting. Get home as quick as you can.'

'Thanks Mister,' yelled George as he ran off back home, his precious bullet in his pocket.

*

He couldn't wait to see Jamal. He was supposed to join him for rice pudding at Uncle Basil's but he was late. George pressed his hand against his jeans, making sure the bullet was there – Jamal was going to be so jealous.

'Uncle, when is Dad coming?' asked George.

'Soon George. Stop pestering me.'

'There won't be a curfew tonight, right uncle?'

'No there won't,' replied Uncle Basil. 'It's Christmas. They've come to an agreement to let people celebrate. We are all going to have dinner later this evening with your aunts and cou...Abu-Fawzeh...What can I do you for?'

George noticed the look of concern on his uncle's face. Abu-Fawzeh had just walked in. George wondered why his uncle looked more nervous than usual, until he spotted the edge of a pistol behind Abu-Fawzeh's jacket.

'I'll have one of those great cocktails you make, Basil, the one with the cranberries and walnuts,' said Abu-Fawzeh. 'And another one for my friend,' he said, while gesturing to a white Subaru parked outside of the shop.

George didn't say anything. This man wasn't a soldier, he was a local -maybe he was one of the rude men that Mom and Dad couldn't stand. George knew better than to ask questions. He could tell Uncle Basil was apprehensive; he worked quicker than usual and spilled some of the milk.

'Here you go Abu-Fawzeh,' said Uncle Basil.

'How much Basil?'

'Nothing, Abu-Fawzeh, it's on us. For your sacrifices.'

'Thank you, Basil. I hope you and your family have a blessed Christmas.'

Abu-Fawzeh walked out towards the white Subaru.

'Uncle Basil…is that man one of th…'

'Shut up,' hissed Uncle Basil, 'Don't ask questions.'

George didn't want to press the matter, he quickly shrugged away the encounter as soon as he realised he had finished his pudding.

'Where is Dad?'

'He's on his way with Elisa, I already told you,' said Uncle Basil.

'You didn't say Elisa was coming, now I have to play stupid girly games with her.'

'Yeah, well, she's your sister, that means she's your responsibility. You ought to take care of her. Anyway, what did you expect? I told you, the whole family is getting together. Your mom is already at Auntie's.'

'I do take care of her. I fight with the boys when they bully her at school.'

'Who are you kidding? You haven't been to school in months, George.'

'Before,' exclaimed George. 'Can I have another rice pudding?'

'No George, don't be greedy. Leave some room for dinner.'

'What if I show you something really cool?'

'What is it?' asked Uncle Basil with a chuckle.

'Pudding first.'

Uncle Basil took out another serving of rice pudding and put it up on the counter. 'I'll tell you what. If it's really that cool, you'll get the rice pudding. So, what is it?'

'A bullet, a really big one, not like the flimsy ones in Abu-Fawzeh's gun.'

'How in God's name do you know about that?'

'Don't be silly Uncle, we find those bullets all the time. I know where they come from!'

'I'm talking about Abu-Fawzeh's gun, George.'

'Oh…I saw it, when he walked in.'

'Listen to me, George,' said Uncle Basil as he edged closer to his nephew and got down to eye level. 'You mustn't tell anyone. You'll put us all in danger if you do. Do you understand?'

'I understand.'

'Promise me George.'

'I Promise.'

'Here's your rice pudding' said Uncle Basil. 'You'd better leave some room for dinner or I won't hear the end of it from your au…'

A torrent of machine gun fire brought their discussion to end. George could tell it was very close. Closer than when the shooting starts near home.

'Stay here,' commanded his uncle as he ran outside. 'Don't you dare leave this shop!'

George reached for the rice pudding. He didn't even have to show Uncle Basil the bullet.

He sat there, enjoying his meal, wondering what was going on. He looked outside and noticed that people were running past the shop, towards the church. What's the harm in seeing what happened?

He made his way out of the shop and followed the commotion. He could hear people yelling and some were even cursing, the kind of words Mom would smack him for saying. He edged through the crowd and spotted the white Subaru at an intersection, riddled with bullets. Around it stood a dozen or so soldiers – I know that voice. Uncle Basil was yelling at the top of his lungs, trying to get past the soldiers who were holding him back.

George edged his way forward, his small frame manoeuvring through the crowd. He saw the soldier from earlier sitting on the pavement, the one with the chiselled face, the one with the scar, Elan; there were tears in his eyes.

'Murderer,' yelled the crowd. 'Son of a bitch!'

On the pavement, adjacent to the Subaru, were two dead bodies. A man, and a little girl. They must've been crossing parallel to the car when they got hit.

Didn't Uncle Basil say Dad was coming with Elisa?

Poetry

Alexander Musleh

Carmina

A prison like no other
It engulfs her slowly, a relentless force
A prison not of walls
Mental blocks penetrate once dreaming thoughts
A play on her psyche, forcing her to dance
Dance to the tune of loss and regret
Dance woefully alongside remorse
Glass slippers forged of broken dreams
As the ballads of misery play their tune
She stops her dance, in pause to think
Apathy, a convenience
To dance in sorrow till the end of time
Or to break out of her prison
To persevere

A Prayer

Despair, a misunderstood concept
Most are mistaken, for they fear what is mortal
That which is corporeal
Yet I dread not the nightly horrors that roam this land
Nor the aggression of my earthly brother
I do not shudder at the thought of genocide
Or at the sight of a mangled child

Yet day by day my chest is heavy
And my body continues to regress
Glass after glass of exotic substances disappear
My mind is numbed, a slight tinge of euphoria
A blurring memory, I begin to forget
Cigarette smoke gracefully conquers my lungs
The smoke, its dance is akin to art
This moment of serenity, I know it will be short-lived
An hour past; it fades, it fades

With sanity comes fear
And though I have lost my faith, I pray
I pray that after I die, I shall simply just die
I care not for an afterlife, nor infinite knowledge
Nor do I pine for infinite bliss
That hollow promise of eternity

Moonshine

For that is my greatest anxiety
An answer to every question
The decay of my will
An everlasting soul, destined to kneel
The fear of immortality, on and on
And on, and on

Forgive me, for I have but one request
If the antithesis of heaven is nihility
Then by all means, I opt to burn in hell

Fuyu

Thea Etnum

(A short story)

(Japan, 19th century)

Tiny steps, following one after the other through snow so thick, almost as hard as ice.

She walks; a thin walk towards a white bridge. Soundless.

There was little trace of her passing through the town of Meguro, making her way from the house of Kimura-sama towards the arched stone of the bridge. Only furtive trails behind her, barely visible, open cuts through bright snow like marks of teeth half sunk into the white flesh of *nashi*…nothing that time wouldn't fill back in, she thought, gazing over her shoulder. There was no emptiness that time could not snow its way into.

Kimura-sama had been drinking melted snow from his crimson cup when she'd slipped out of his house with her white paper umbrella and that white bundle. He always drank melted snow from Fuji-san, cold water between his sips of *osake*, burning hot. Hot and cold, his drinks; hot and cold, his gaze. But he had kept his word; he, a client of the pleasure quarter, a rough merchant, had paid her family's debt so that she could stop working as a *yūjo*, and he had married her. So now, she obeyed him. But a life with her new husband was in no way easier than what she'd had before – just different.

She held the white bundle tightly against her chest, felt its strange weight pressing, pulling, like that of a bronze statue.

Her first steps across the bridge of Meguro felt heavy; all the rest to follow, all the heavier. But they served her well, taking her towards the coldest night about to cross her path. It would meet her at the other end of the bridge, together with the half-cut moon above the rising hill, and a distant, solitary walker with a hat as wide as the Chinese map of the sky.

The snow felt like silk, almost slipping from underneath her feet as she was trying to get further and further away from her home; but never far enough, never truly away. No running, she whispered to herself; there was no running from your own body, only with it, within it.

And it was all, all that was her life, from and of the body; the tired body, pulling onwards, labouring, moving, inventing gestures, strong or vile or delicate. Her own moves through mounting snow, delicate; a girl's moves always had to be delicate, that's what she'd been told as a child, and pain was never an excuse. She stepped over the bridge, her useless pain spreading inside her like red ink on thin rice paper.

Her fingers tensed, contracting from the cold outside, or from the unhealed ache, or from that sense of sorrow as she was holding part of herself against herself, the small body of her first child. Breathless.

Kimura-sama had not wanted that child: 'We will give back the thing that you have given birth to,' he'd said. She did not argue. It was not the time to raise a prematurely born girl, when there was work to be done. Had it been a boy, things could have been different; a boy might have been of help. 'Give it back to the unborn. We have no life for it here.' Kimura-sama had told the midwife, so that old woman with blackened teeth had bathed the child, put it to sleep, never to wake again.

She'd only heard her baby crying once, a strange cry, strong, like the scream of a crane about to fly off; then silenced. She had told the midwife not to take the body. The mother would be the one to take it, unseen, gentle, wrapping a piece of cloth around the box the midwife had put it in; trying to tie a double knot on top with trembling fingers, again and again, until it was finally done.

And then, she had walked.

She had walked towards the drum bridge, and over it, stopping at the highest point of stone and snow; she stopped, but the snow did not, the hours did not. The river did not. And even in the dark, she could see its liquid blue undulations as she peered over her left shoulder to the wavering water; water to drop that small body into... she imagined its soul slipping away like white koi, then going as deep down as it would like to go, shining like mirrors sinking to the bottom. She would pray for the frail spirit of the child to flow with the river, away from the bridge, as far away from that bridge as possible, to a new life. It was said there was another life for the soul, a better one, one that it might inhabit together with the new skin it would take on... but there was no way of knowing.

She had never seen a night like that. There would never be another like it. The silk of tight clothing to hide the skin in layers and layers, just like the silk of snow was hiding the earth away, numbing. She bent, feeble, unwell, and in her near fall, stretched out her hand to clasp the wooden bar of the bridge. The bundle, that little bundle, fell in the snow. White on white, it could barely be seen.

She was quick to pick up what she'd dropped, then got up and faced the river. What helped the soul release the burden of an unlived life, she wondered. Was it the water streaming down, renewing itself in its flow? Was it the fire to purify, the earth to swallow and transform? Which rite of those she knew was the right one, what would help more? And did rites even help at all? The image of the god to guide the souls of children came to her tired mind – she'd seen his statue at the crossroads, or next to silent temples... she could invoke his name, OJizō-sama; and then the name of Nembutsu. That, she could do.

She watched soft flakes, sifting in silence. So terrible they were. So terrible it was; that unknown greed of all things delicate, as they so quickly perished.

Then, she got closer to the margin.

No one around her; no one to see how, through all the speckled whiteness drifting from up to down and melting upon the water, another thing was falling, a small white bundle, dropped into the river by her shaking hands.

The seed that would not grow would be removed; the seedling that did not thrive would be pulled out and left to die. That was the soul of the very world, but the river knew how to move freely through it – that's why she'd chosen it. She knew of many others that had done the same before her.

Almost the hour of the boar it was, the hour for her to step down from the drum bridge. She bowed to the river.

After her climb, there came a descent.

Now, she felt twice as heavy.

Now that it was all done, she did not want to return.

Tales of the Void

Thea Etnum

(A short story)

My chest is slowly turning into a cavity, a hole. I am a vessel about to be drained; a body with no blood, no organs, no life. I can feel this strange void spreading like a black hole inside my thorax, from the chest to the abdomen.

I don't know what I can do to stop this. I can't hold on to anything anymore; names, faces, memories, thoughts – all is fading, vanishing. This is the curse of my void.

Before it all began, I used to see my soul in night dreams. A soul like a totem that was forever changing shape; one second, it was a slithering snake about to bite its own tail. Then, it turned into a frightening hound, howling for the lives that it had lost, and the one that it was about to lose. It was the memory of blood, seething, that had stirred it up – but I thought my soul-beast would know that there was no blood in the land of shadows, that realm it would escape to every night. And from that land, it would always find its way back to me. Until one night, not that long ago, when my soul decided not to return.

And that's how it started – I lost a first part of myself to the void and gained the smaller parts, the strange bits and pieces of a tainted world that contaminated my reality.

I've been unable to sleep ever since. I thought dreams only happened when you slept, until they started dripping, then pouring, into my surrounding reality. Or is it that my reality has turned into a dream, one of spreading emptiness?

I hoped there might be something, a cure that someone in the waking world could give me. So, I thought I'd ask them, the doctors and nurses, to help me stop the cavity from opening wider. All they could do was give advice, all they had for me were words. So, I took their advice, and went to find their recommended cures for my strange disease. I got lost among the tall stands of a small pharmacy and felt little hope as I heard that question again:

'How may I help you?'

'I'll show you,' I said to the young pharmacist who'd asked. I pulled my shirt up and opened up my ribs and my abdomen like the panels of a triptych. She watched and smiled in silence.

'Oh. Have you been to the doctor? I would need to see your diagnosis... but don't worry; we have cures for just about everything here.' She then smiled almost lovingly at the shelves behind me, as if they were human.

I stretched out my arms to her, opened my palms and confessed. 'It is all here, on my hands. You see, I forget and lose almost everything. This hole –' we both looked down at the cavity in my chest. 'It's a symptom... I can't keep anything I'm given, but I have written what the doctors said on my hands. Perhaps you could read my diagnosis?'

'Of course. But you should close yourself up now,' she frowned while gazing at the small black letters on my palms. 'We wouldn't want you to scare off the other customers.' She then read a few words of my jumbled diagnosis, trying to make some sense of it all. I withdrew my palms, but she kept on repeating those medical terms until they became incoherent, almost as if she were speaking in tongues.

'You should stop now,' I told her and echoed her words. 'You wouldn't want to scare off the other customers.'

'How do I do that?' she asked, gaze locked on the place where my hands had been. 'How do I stop?'

'I don't know...'

'They're your words, written on your hands. You should know. Please tell me how to stop. Please.'

I left. I left her next to her beloved stands, saying the same things over and over again. But somewhere along the way I had forgotten how to close my thorax, so I kept walking around with an open ribcage like two ill-grown flesh wings on either side of a spreading cavity. I'd begun losing hope; I couldn't contain anything anymore, not even the simple knowledge of how to close myself up again.

'How can you expose yourself like that? You are disgusting,' a girl said in the park next to the pharmacy. 'No,' I whispered to her. 'I'm just empty.' *What use for the blind to cover their eyes?* I thought.

'I pity you,' said a tall, elderly woman walking a few metres behind the girl, who had now quickened her step. The woman stopped her shopping trolley, took off her cat's-eye sunglasses and lit up a cigarette. Her smudged eyeliner made her dark eyes look like holes.

'You are worse off than I am,' she pondered and exhaled a slim wisp of smoke. 'Here, have this.'

She took off her small red scarf, asked me to turn around, and closed me up from behind, gently, with hands as cold as dawn, and wrapped the piece of silk around me, pulling tightly, pulling it like a corset.

I let her, but I told her it wouldn't do me any good, it wouldn't last. All of a sudden, her touch began to burn. I turned around, only to see that the bleach-blonde curls all around her wrinkled face had been set ablaze. Her hair had gone up in a swirling flame, burning like a torch – so brightly that her features became indistinguishable. I knew I couldn't be around her for long. I couldn't even look at her, so I ran away, praying that she would not burn to death. Though I knew her burning would not consume all of her at once. Her curse took its time, just like mine. But I, for one, was running out of time.

I knew there was a river somewhere, I longed for the relief of cool water after the smouldering heat of those flames.

'How can you walk around like that?' a man asked when he saw me sat by the side of the river. His eyes, too, were tinged with pity as he noticed the scarf wrapped around my broken body. Under that hot sun, he was wearing a white fur coat.

'I could ask you the same question,' I smiled.

'Here,' he said, and took off his coat. Before I could tell him that I didn't want it, he put it on my shoulders, with moves as fast as a predator's. The moment it touched me, it felt cold, ice cold.

'Please, take it off,' I begged. But it was too late. It fell from my hot shoulders like snow off the eaves of a roof.

'I only wanted to help you,' he murmured.

'It's not you,' I smiled at him. 'It's me... sorry, I have destroyed your coat.'

'Don't worry.' He sat down next to me and whispered. 'Nothing is lost, nothing is created...'

'Everything is transformed,' I continued.

I could barely utter those words, when he plunged into the river below. I closed my eyes in fear and when I opened them, all I saw were the swollen waters of a river that had turned glistening white.

It was right then and there that I promised myself I wouldn't ask for help or take anything from anyone ever again. I would stop asking, I would stop hoping, I would stop searching. I would allow the void to have its way.

I peered at the pile of snow, all that was left of the man's coat, and walked away. But it wasn't long before I felt that I was being followed. I looked over my shoulder and saw the supple body of a mysterious four-legged animal coming towards me, white like the snow that had now disappeared completely, as if it was made of that very snow. The creature and I stared at each other, and there was nothing but silence between and around us. A strange silence, one that the quiet animal would not break.

'Go away,' I said. 'Go away, before you become like me. Before something happens to you.'

But the moment I turned around, I knew it would follow. Even now, I don't know why it won't go its own way. Perhaps it can smell the flesh that the hole is eating away at. But when I look at its steel-coloured eyes, I think that, maybe, it is just like me – maybe it's just forgotten its way and is tired of searching. So now, we are lost together.

When I stop, the white creature stops, but it never comes too close. It keeps its careful distance. We have been walking aimlessly, perhaps for a day, perhaps for a year.

I gaze at the sun. It is only getting bigger, like the void inside. The brighter its blaze, the more tired I become. My eyelids feel heavy, I need to lie down and I know it won't be long until it all ends. I close my eyes and lie on my back under the sun at zenith. The animal is approaching; it's never gotten this close to me before. I feel its cold breath as it sniffs my decaying body, its fangs as it rips away the scarf. I always knew I would lose that scarf, just as I know that predators give in to the smell of dried blood and flesh. I should be afraid of what is about to happen, I should feel terror at the thought that all that will be left of me is naked bones after a violent feast.

But there's no violence in this. No hunger for a white animal stepping inside an open ribcage. The cavity has been spreading, it is now wide enough to let the supple creature nestle inside the carving of my void, and I know that I will soon slip into sleep just as softly…just as quietly…

As I lie on the ground, I can feel my soul returning to me.

The Unnamed

Thea Etnum

(A novel extract)

Sirale had never given me the key to his white stone cabin at the foot of the volcano. He would always be the one to let me in, opening the slim-frame door of the entrance and then silently withdrawing behind it. As he almost vanished inside the protective womb of a round and damp room, among narrow shelves crammed with vials and bottles, I was fascinated by the reflection of his silhouette sliding like a liquid shadow, a dark serpent slithering along all those translucent surfaces. I would try to move around that space quietly, almost as quietly as Sirale's reflection, showing the greatest care so as not to upset his unusually sensitive hearing.

For years, I had been going to that small cabin. I had been there day by day, to assist Sirale and to learn from him, with unwavering punctuality. On that morning in June, right after the summer solstice, I had once again arrived on time; but when I knocked, there was no answer. That's when I knew with discomforting certainty that Sirale had gone.

Many a time that pale blue door had opened right in front of me, before I'd even touched it, just as I'd been approaching the cabin, crushing the dark gravel and volcanic sand of the winding path underneath my feet.

'I can hear your footsteps from houses away,' Sirale had said weeks, if not days, before that morning. 'Your heavy footsteps.'

'I seldom come here unburdened. You always ask me to bring more and more material for our experiments,' I'd replied, just as I'd been taking the pieces of stone and metal out of my sack to arrange them in their corresponding places on the shelves.

'You walk in the same way every time, even when you do not need to bring anything.'

I hadn't asked him about the meaning of those words, but they stayed with me, stirring my thoughts, like most of the things he had said, and all of the things he had taught me – preparing cures and recipes, mixing salts, oils, pigments. And then the other lessons too, 'the higher teachings', as he would call them, about the essence of things, transformation… the ones that he had shown me so little of.

I took the sack, with the rocks and the salts I'd been carrying with me, off my shoulders, and let it fall to the ground; a single strong thud reminding me that I could count on the same, solid earth to support the weight of everything – yet somehow, I just couldn't feel it. I regained my senses the moment I noticed that beams had been nailed to the small windows, shutting the cabin completely, making it impenetrable. *This house is now just like his heart,* I'd thought.

'He's dead.' It was a strange whisper; a child's voice, soft, but unsettling. I turned around. Sheathed in her mother's golden shawl, Marina the zingara child was unrecognizable – a familiar stranger eyeing me through my deepest confusion, my overwhelming desolation.

'The old man smelled like the volcano mud baths,' she continued in the same hushed tone. 'He smelled of death, that's what Mamma said.'

I stared at Marina and realised she must've been following me around for quite some time. She'd inherited more than her mother's piercing dark gaze – her words were usually the very echo of the gypsy woman's often careless speech and blunt judgment. Though I understood what the child was referring to – that ever-present odour of sulphur and salts on Sirale's clothes, the one that never really faded, which I had lost all sensitivity towards, was considered odd, even terrible, by many of the village.

Marina's words had brought me some solace, since I knew they couldn't have been true. Whatever the reason behind Sirale's unexpected disappearance, death would have had nothing to do with it. My certainty of that came from an inner place beyond reason and doubt, an intuition that shone a bit of light unto the mystery of his disappearance.

'What do you know about death, Marina?' I whispered back, trying to imitate her childish gloomy tone. She grinned at me, her big dark eyes gleaming.

'I know.'

Forgive me, I thought, and made a step towards her. I felt ashamed for having asked her that question – of course she knew, and probably better than most people, myself included. Marina ran towards me and caught my hand, inquisitive and comforting at first, until her grip tightened with impatience and wild curiosity.

'Did he leave with the silver and gold you two were making? Tell me.'

'Why do you ask about things that could not possibly be of interest to a child such as yourself? Tell me.'

Her smile met mine, together with my absolute silence. She then let go of my hand and ran in front of me, setting herself up as a human obstacle of dark curls and frayed golden cloth, resting her small hands on her hips.

'I want to know more… like you do.'

Her lampblack eyes glimmered again, but then she quickly lowered her head to hide her avid look and flushed cheeks. Whilst peering at the leather sandals that she was wearing, much too big for her feet, Marina asked the question I dared not ask myself...

'What are you going to do now that he's gone?'

In the sting of unwanted clarity brought about by her words, I could see everything – all that had been at the foot of the volcano since forever, an entire landscape that I had been crossing for so long, it had, at some obscure point, ceased to truly exist for me. The short brick houses spread out unevenly, many of them abandoned, grey – ruins. A world of stone built upon stone, levelled terraces and dark-leaved shrubs that did not thirst for water. And that one distant well, hidden in the shadow of the taller trees, around their supple roots, interlacing, menacing, part of a dry, austere landscape. Nobody would need that well anymore, I realized and I felt, for the second time in my strange life, abandoned.

'I don't know,' I answered, and I took Marina in my arms, covering her head with the golden cloth. I felt she'd grown a bit taller, a bit heavier than the last time I'd held her.

'Keep your shawl on your head, Marina. The sun is really bright today, this might not be good for you.' Her face became so serious when she heard me saying that; it no longer seemed to be that of a child. As she stood there, in my arms, I was holding all that she would ever be, the very essence of who she was.

'You can make me better if I get sick, no? … If I keep this on my head, will you take your hood off?'

'You know the answer to that, don't you?' She knew it, and yet she would always ask. She nodded and frowned again.

'Then I don't want it like this.' She had let the shawl slip onto her shoulders, while her small left hand rested, abnormally cold, on my hot cheek. 'Don't worry, please,' she smiled sweetly. 'It's good that the old Arab is gone. You can play with me now. You can show me what he's shown you, teach me what he's taught you… you won't leave, will you?'

'I don't know… let's go, I'll take you back to the village. I want to talk to your mother, Marina – is Gina at home?'

'I don't know – that's all you're saying. Well, I don't know, either. I don't know if Mamma is at home,' she mumbled, upset that I couldn't tell her what she would've liked to hear. 'But we can go see. Together.'

I held the child tighter as her thin arms locked around my neck, and carried her out of the blaze and on to the shadows of the footpath. The sun seemed to be disturbing me more than it did Marina, but it could never have hurt me as much as it would have her.

She had become my load on the way back to the village, her body heavier than my morning sack. I left on the same narrow path I'd arrived on. It would have been easier for both me and the child if I would have put her down, easier and cooler, but I did not want to unburden myself. The load made me stronger.

Leaves of tall trees cast myriads of shadows on Marina's bronze forehead and temple. Walking felt like swaying, and my movement brought everything with it: the heat of the summer sun that was making the air thick and dry, the scent of the fading orange blossoms, dust and grains of sand, fine, golden particles rising through slim light beams – my unsettling thoughts, agitated, sifted through the odd hours of that bright morning.

The heat of the sun was slowly becoming that of the body. I barely noticed when Marina's head rested heavy on my shoulder as if she were about to slip into sleep. Her half-closed eyes had turned into narrow streaks of white. Her body tensed, arched and bent. It turned rigid, then all of a sudden furious, like the waves of illness that had once again begun to rise through it. I fell to the ground; I was holding her head with one hand, her body with the other, and realized that what I could have given her to help her was now out of my reach.

The Beautiful Death of Lady Butterfly

Missy Reddy

(A short story extract)
Characters inspired by the music and lyrics of Roger Glover's
Rock Opera 'The Butterfly Ball'.

Lady Butterfly raises her delicate skirts as she draws a breath in, and lowers them as she breathes out. One more breath in and, maintaining the strength of her core, she lifts her feet. She is in flight. A picture of kaleidoscopic beauty, red chiffon blowing in the breeze. How powerful is She that can control the elements with her wings. Yet how blind are her eyes that cannot see. Click, click. She has been tracked. The bat takes a deathly plunge from high up in the tree. His wings, four times the span of hers, beat down on the air. She senses the threat. Her wings beat harder, his do too. He lets out a warning shriek, she already knows her fate. She is between his jaws, his wings beating down on her, she is between two worlds now, red ribbons streaming into the dusk, her core plummets to the ground. It was the most beautiful death that Artemis had ever seen.

*

Hortensia admired her image in the glass. She was a woman of great vision and she was a vision to behold. Her dress was, as always, as black as her hair. A web of lace with gold and silver beads tumbled down one shoulder, meeting her prominent cleavage, and then snaked across one hip and down to a delicate thigh. A break in her skirt revealed a black and red hourglass tattoo at the top of a long sleek leg. Following that leg down, the same lace and beads adorned stiletto heels, sharp to the touch. Following those legs back up, all the way up to her face: as Yin does to Yang, so her shaped brows did contrast with the outline of her eyes, with glittering gold and silver finishing off the lids. Deep green pools for eyes and blood red lips; she was her own masterpiece. Her hair completed her look in that ruffled unruffled way that is perfect only in its disarray.

A dark entity swooped onto the balcony before her eyes and her meditation was broken. Hortensia watched each deathly contortion of the beast, a pain she knew well, the tearing apart of the flesh in a frantic attempt to escape from confinement, so fierce yet so vulnerable. The pushing outwards, the pulling inwards, the twisting and turning, the sickness, she saw it all. And then the transformation process slowed down, the air around the beast began to settle, the black wings folded back to reveal what she'd been waiting for: a man, in the flesh. He slowly rose from one knee to tower above her. And yet it was She who commanded him. With lowered head, he said 'It's done.'

Hortensia nodded. 'Very well then.' She reached slowly between her breasts, lingered a moment seeing how he watched her hand hungrily, longingly. It pleased her. From the wildness in his eyes, she could see that it wasn't the thought of the payment that held him captivated, but the chance of an encounter with her; easing the pain of his transformation. But not tonight. She slowly withdrew her hand, tormenting him a little more. She pulled out a small purse and proffered it to him. His gaze dropped to the ground. She tracked the line of his gaze with pleasure: her eyes; a final plea, her breasts; one last look. He licked his lips, breathed in and breathed out. Pursing his lips, he relented and took the money.

'Now, away!' she commanded fiercely, casting him a threatening look straight in his eyes, and slammed the balcony door. The impact was too great for the glass and a wave of cracks appeared over its pane. Through the cracks, Hortensia could see the dark figure retreating over the balcony and into the night, still in human form; one could not attempt a second transformation so soon after the first. Hortensia shifted her focus to her own image; even more pleasing to her now it was distorted by the broken glass. She smiled and closed the blinds.

*

Saffron cleaned the whole cottage before a big event. 'Lift your feet Tom, come on, up.' She attacked Tom's feet with the vacuum cleaner. She was a small, stocky woman. The homely type.

He threw her a befuddled scowl. 'Do you have to, love?' She was disturbing his quiet read.

'Yes Tom, I do have to. It's Lady Butterfly.' Nothing was getting in the way of her big clean.

'It's a TV programme, love, why do you have to tidy for a TV programme?'

He'd never really understood her, he was a newspaper man, she was a TV lady, never the twain shall meet. 'I'm going to ignore you Tom, I'm not going to let you spoil it for me.' Back in the early days she would have risen to such bait. She went into the kitchen, retrieved a bottle of red wine and two glasses. She placed them on the table beside the settee where Tom was sitting with his newspaper. Still standing, she poured herself a glass. 'I hope you're not planning on sitting here and rustling that paper all the way through my show'.

*

Raif was striding up and down his dressing room, preparing to host the late night show. He wore his best waistcoat; printed in an array of brightly coloured horizontal diamonds. His yellow cravat billowed out of his deep V neck, like the plume of a perverse bird. A matching yellow handkerchief cascaded from a pocket at his waist. His trousers were identical to the waistcoat in their magnificent print. He was indeed a dapper gent; tall and slender with a spring in his step. He stopped for a moment to check out his reflection in the mirror. He was proud of his long mousy hair that defied his age in its thickness and lustre. He waved his head from side to side, reminding himself of a swanky Afghan hound. 'Awooo.' He chuckled. A multitude of thin creases appeared around his eyes. He leaned into the mirror to take a closer look. The lines, his reddened cheeks, and deep shadows under his eyes, were the distinctive markings of a middle-aged man who'd had more than his fair share of late nights and thrills. He carefully applied another layer of powder and turned his back on the mirror. Removing a small black cylinder from his trouser pocket, he took a sniff in each nostril. A little pick me up. Never mind. He took a few more steps, as best he could in such a small room. Lifting his chin up, he took a breath in, and stretched out his arms. He breathed out as he lowered his arms to his sides. That's better. 'Tonight will be the most marvellous night of all,' he declared, flashing his best smile back at the mirror.

*

Artemis awoke from his stasis; a ritual that had been steadily increasing in regularity since he'd started to take the pills. Through the window of his den, his sleepy eyes were drawn to a beautiful naked man walking through the moonlit woods. Artemis had been unable to take his human form for many months now, but even then he had been small and unimpressive when compared to this tall man; rippling waves of muscle, accentuated by the moonlight. Artemis crept towards the corner of the window. Besides the man's bodily beauty, there was something else that captured Artemis' attention. The man seemed to be engaged in a curious activity; hands in front of his eyes, inspecting something, counting small objects; coins perhaps. Artemis watched as the man cast a larger object away from himself into the bushes.

Waiting until he was sure the man had passed, Artemis proceeded to the rough area where he'd seen the object thrown. He scrabbled through the bushes and sifted through bits of leaf, twig, moss and dirt until he found something that was alien to its surroundings; it was stiff and smooth. Out from the bushes, he held the object up in the moonlight and could see he'd obtained a small leather purse. He could just about make out a strange marking on the purse, like an hourglass. The sickness was already starting to creep up on him; the moments of pain-free lucidity were becoming shorter and he wondered if one day they would cease altogether. Artemis retreated to his den to find a pill that would both relieve his suffering and render him unconscious for the next number of hours.

Artemis opened his pill box and pulled out a red and white striped capsule. With the pill in one paw and the purse in the other, Artemis recalled something else that had fallen that night; the body of a butterfly stripped of its wings.

The Collection

Missy Reddy

(A short story extract)

'Seems like a pretty regular suicide to me,' concluded Sam; forty-something, acts like he's twenty-something, handsome in his own way, Erica supposed.

'I'd agree Sam, but let's go through the correct procedure okay?' said Erica; thirty-something, acts thirty-something, maybe older, definitely older than Sam though.

Sam rolled his eyes at Erica. She frowned and set her briefcase down on the dining room table, ignoring Sam's childish posturing. Erica's classic brown leather briefcase had been a present from her father when she'd joined the police force. She had felt that it was an odd present to give a trainee police constable but she'd accepted it graciously nonetheless. It had remained in the back of her cupboard for at least a decade before she'd pulled it out and dusted it down. And now it was like another limb to her; she wondered how she'd ever managed without it. Erica carefully thumbed in the combination codes and pressed the two gold clasps to open the briefcase, click click, *that* sound and the familiar scent of paper and leather emanating from the case made her smile. Erica's paperwork was neatly organised in plastic folders in the main compartment of the briefcase. She removed one of the folders, and a clipboard from a pocket in the lid of the briefcase.

'Right, here we go, the incident report.' She attached the report template to her clipboard. Erica read aloud the first heading on the report: 'Brief description of setting.'

Through the large bay windows, Erica could see that the streetlamps were on. A number of tall trees and a few parked cars lined an otherwise quiet street. From the decor inside the dining room, it was clear that the man who had lived here had a passion for antique wooden furniture; the dining room table and chairs, a tall dresser, a gold framed mirror and picture frames. There were no signs of anything modern in this room.

'Middle-class gaff out in arty farty suburbia?' Sam offered. He grinned, childlike dimples appearing around the corners of his mouth.

Erica frowned and focused on the report, 'How about: Victorian mid terrace in small suburb of Upford?' It wasn't really a question. Erica moved on, 'Brief description of incident.'

'Old dude found swinging from the rafters. Possible motive? Too old, can't get laid.'

Erica glared at Sam as he smiled again, running his fingers through his thick blonde hair, head nodding away in amusement like one of those irritating dogs. He was completely incapable of taking anything seriously in this world. Erica could see how it worked for Sam, as a strategy to manage the emotional demands of the job. But it meant it was quite impossible, when partnered up with him, to get anything done.

'How about: Neighbour alerted the police of an unusual absence of activity at the premises for circa four to five days. DC Samuel Milner and DS Erica Van Hoesen attended the premises. IC1 middle-aged man circa 65 years of age found suspended from a ceiling joist–'

'What was wrong with *the rafters*?'

'Okay, suspended from the rafters.' Erica wrote *ceiling joist*. She continued, 'in the attic by the medium of a... What do you think the diameter of the rope is?'

'Diameter?' Sam asked.

'How thick is it?'

'It says *brief* description.'

'Alright, by the medium of a rope attached to his neck.' Erica would check the rope diameter later when she got a chance. She continued to read aloud as she wrote, ensuring Sam was involved in the process. 'A small wooden stool was found overturned at the man's feet.' She would check the dimensions of *that* later too. 'DC Samuel Milner–'

'That's me.'

'–checked for a pulse on discovery of the man at three minutes past twenty-one hundred hours–'

'But he was already a stiffy,' Sam said, impatiently.

'Sam, come on, bear with me; it won't take long if we work together on this.' Erica glanced at her watch. Ten forty. It *was* getting late.

'It's boring, let's get out of here and head to the pub, we can finish the paperwork over a nice cold beer.'

Erica continued, 'The man had already entered a state of advanced rigor mortis; suggesting he'd been dead for circa–'

'There it is again.'

Erica ignored Sam's remark. Knowing he hated the use of jargon, she emphasised it all the more, 'circa 12 to 24 hours.'

'Great! Pub?' Sam closed Erica's briefcase and, taking it in one hand, escorted Erica out of the dining room with the other, clipboard and pen still poised.

Erica noted the continuation of the antique theme in the hallway as Sam led her past a small wooden French dresser. She looked Sam in the eyes. 'Would you agree we carried out a full search of the house?'

'Yes.' Sam turned the brass handle and opened the front door, letting in the lure of the early-autumn air.

'And we checked there were no signs of forced entry?'

'Yes.' Sam escorted Erica out of the front door, closed it behind them and led Erica down the steps.

'There was nothing suspicious looking about the house or anything was there?'

'No.' Sam opened the passenger door of his black Audi cabriolet for Erica. How he could afford such a vehicle on a DC's salary was beyond her. She certainly couldn't have afforded one herself. Unless this was also his home. Erica chuckled inwardly and lowered herself into the comfortable leather passenger seat. Sam popped her briefcase in the boot and quickly walked round to his side. He slipped in behind the wheel and started the engine before Erica could ask any further questions.

'Okay Sam, you win. I'll quickly call the undertakers to let them know we're finished at the house. We can complete the paperwork down the pub, I guess.'

*

'Glad we're out of there,' Sam said as he and Erica walked through the doors of *The Rising Sun*. 'That place was freaking me out. What can I get ya?' He gestured to the bar.

'Just a tonic water for me thanks Sam.'

'Gin and tonic it is then.'

'Alright, just the one.' Erica proceeded to a discreet corner of the pub, where they might continue their work.

'Erica, over here, by the fire,' Sam called, drinks in hand. It was a little more central than she'd have liked but it was quiet in the pub tonight, so she relented.

Erica sat down on a small leather sofa facing the fireplace, sinking down further than she'd expected. She yawned and then attempted a more upright sitting position. Erica gazed at the fireplace. She could see straight through it to the other side of the pub. How efficient, heating both sides of the building at the same time. Above the fireplace was a red-brick chimney breast reaching up to a cream ceiling and wooden beams. There was a deer's head on a plaque about halfway down the chimney breast. Sam sat down right next to Erica though there were plenty of other empty chairs that he could have occupied. He was no friend of personal space. He put the drinks down on the low oval table in front of them.

Erica laid her briefcase down on the table, opened it and pulled out the paperwork.

'Have a drink first.' Sam handed Erica a short glass containing a clear liquid, and started to sip his pint of dark ale.

'What are you drinking Sam?'

'It's called *Sheep Shagger*, but before you say it, I'm not.'

Erica chuckled and took a sip of her drink, 'Cor Sam, is that a double?' She put the paperwork back in the briefcase.

'Yeah, thought you needed it after a day like today.'

'Thanks, it was a bit of a stonker wasn't it?' She took another sip. The strength of the drink made her wince. She put down the glass and retrieved the paperwork again, returning to her work. 'So do we know who he was then? You took the call.'

'The neighbour said he was a psychologist or psychiatrist, something like that,' Sam said.

'Damn shrinks!' It was a snap judgement and Erica blushed. Sam looked at her, surprised. 'Sorry, I just don't get it. They're meant to help others. They're not meant to be the sick ones, are they?'

'Okay, well that's what he was. He'd split up with his wife a couple of years ago apparently.'

They looked at each other and said, almost in unison, 'Messy divorce.' They'd seen it before. In fact, they'd seen more than their fair share of suicides over the last eight years since they'd been partners.

Holding her paperwork on her lap with one hand, Erica leaned forward and picked up her drink. This time she took a large swig and shuddered. She looked up at the deer's head. 'Do you think that's real?'

'I don't really know; it looks kind of old.'

The fur was worn in places but it was the eyes that took Erica's interest. 'It seems to be looking right at me.'

Erica continued to gaze at the deer. Suddenly, Sam grabbed her shoulder with both hands, as if to make her jump. She did indeed jump. And so did her glass, and what remained of her drink happily permeated the paperwork in her lap. 'Shit Sam, what did you do that for?'

'Shit, sorry Erica.' He proceeded to the bar while Erica grabbed a handful of napkins from the dumbwaiter at the side of the fireplace. She carefully mopped up the spillage on the paperwork. It was lucky it had been the gin and tonic that had spilt, not the dark ale, or they may have had to start all over again. Erica carefully put the paperwork back in her briefcase and closed the lid. She took the briefcase off the table and placed it down by her legs. Sam arrived back with two more drinks.

'Oh, I thought you were just going to get something to clear up the mess. It's done now anyway.' Erica took the short glass from Sam, 'Alright, one more drink.' He slumped next to her once again, pint in hand. She took a sip from her glass. 'Another double?'

'Only to replace the one I spilt. Now, where were we?' Sam looked around for the paperwork.

'The deer's head?' Erica smiled. 'I've put the report away now; I'll finish it later. I'll call you if I need any more info.' She unsecured the clip that had been holding her long brown mane at bay all day and gently ruffled her hair. She relaxed back into her chair and sipped her drink. Sam smiled, once again revealing the dimples on his rugged cheeks.

⋆

Erica was sitting in her small office at the police station, having one of her ever-increasing paper pushing days. She sighed and looked at the neat piles she'd carefully arranged on her desk that morning but, to be fair, hardly made a mark on since. The room was otherwise quite sparse; a row of shelves above her desk housed some out-of-date policy and procedure manuals; an unused filing cabinet gathered dust; everything was stored centrally these days.

The phone rang, a light relief from the starkness of procrastination. Erica lifted the receiver, 'Van Hoesen,' she said flatly.

'Cheer up Erica, you've got a visitor.'

'Alright Debs, I'll be out in a minute.'

Erica stood up from her chair and brushed down her skirt. It would help her mood if the room had some external light, she felt. All that connected her with the outside world, during these long administrative days, was a small internal window overlooking a corridor illuminated by strip lighting. Otherwise, the room was basically a broom cupboard. She gladly opened the office door, immediately feeling the change in humidity, as if stepping out of an unlocked safe. She secured the office door behind her and proceeded through the hallway and down the stairs to reception. She wasn't expecting any visitors today but it was a welcome relief from those four walls.

Erica scanned the row of chairs in front of the reception counter. First, an officer handcuffed to a young lad; unlikely to be for her. Next, a little old lady clutching a small brown leather handbag. Maybe. And then there was a middle-aged woman with a short bob of dark brown hair and a worried look on her face. She was holding what seemed to be a notebook on her lap. Erica looked at Debs and discretely gestured to the middle-aged woman, Debs nodded, so Erica made her approach.

'Good afternoon, I'm Detective Sergeant Erica Van Hoesen, I believe you're here to see me.'

'Mrs Virginia Greaves,' the woman said. Erica searched her mind for a connection to that name. Oh yes, Edward Greaves; Erica had filed that case for closure a few weeks ago. 'I've got something I think you need to see,' Mrs Greaves said, looking down at the notebook.

'Alright Mrs Greaves, you'd better come with me.' Erica looked back at the reception desk. 'Debs, are any of the interview rooms free?' she asked.

'Yes, room six.' Debs handed Erica a pair of green gloves and a plastic evidence bag.

'Great, we'll be in there.' Erica led Mrs Greaves down a long corridor to the left of the reception desk. About halfway down the corridor on the right-hand side, they found their room. 'Here we are.' Erica opened the door for Mrs Greaves. Mrs Greaves sat down on one side of the small table in the centre of the room and Erica sat down opposite her. 'You have something to show me, Mrs Greaves?' Erica gestured to the notebook.

'Virginia, please.' Erica nodded. Virginia began. 'I was clearing a few things out from my ex-husband's house, preparing for the sale and all after his, well, death.' Erica's thoughts travelled back to the house, the antique furniture, the man hanging there in his attic, and then the deer's head in the pub afterwards. She remembered coming into the office the next day, with a slightly muggy head from one too many gin and tonics the night before, and completing the paperwork alone. Virginia continued. 'And I found this… journal. I don't really know what to make of it, but I thought you ought to see it, in case, you know, in case it meant anything, I don't suppose it is anything really.'

The journal was a simple A5 spiral-bound book with a brown leather cover and an elastic strap to secure its contents. Erica slipped on the green plastic gloves and opened the first page. There was a photo of a young woman, possibly in her 20s. She had long blonde hair and was dressed in a skirt and blouse; attire you'd expect of an office worker. She sat at a desk looking directly at the camera and wore a demure corporate expression.

Erica looked at Virginia. 'Do you know this woman?' She thought it may have been a daughter or niece.

'No I don't,' Virginia replied. 'Or the others. We've been divorced for two years now, so it's... you know... it's…' She sighed. 'I only looked at the journal because I thought it might have been one of our old holiday journals. It fell out from behind the chest in the hallway.'

'The chest?' Erica asked. Sam and Erica had done a thorough search of the house but they hadn't thought to look behind the little French dresser, or any of the other furniture really; it wasn't common practice in these seemingly straightforward cases.

'Yes, I was going to take it with me. But I didn't. I mean, it was his in the end. Anyway, it isn't that; I'm not sentimental.' Virginia gestured at the journal. 'After two years he's entitled to move on isn't he? I have; in a way. It just doesn't make sense – all these girls?'

Erica continued to look through the journal. There were numerous photos of young women. In some pictures, the women were smiling at the camera, but other pictures were more obscure. There was a photo of a woman walking through a car park that looked as though it had been taken from a first-floor window. Another picture, of a woman sitting in an office engaged in conversation, seemed to have been taken through the crack of a door.

Virginia continued to talk as Erica scoured the pages. 'Edward used to make a holiday journal each year, sticking in photos, tickets et cetera… but not like this… all this other stuff.'

There were indeed other items stuck neatly to the pages. Odd intimate objects. What appeared to be fingernail clippings. A hair band with some strands of red hair. A tissue that looked as though it had been used to blot lipstick. A lolly stick. A cigarette butt. One would imagine that the ordinary person would want to throw this kind of thing out; not stick it in a journal.

There were some handwritten entries in the book too. Erica gestured to a small passage of writing. 'And this?'

'That's my husband's handwriting,' Virginia confirmed. 'So what do you think? It's a bit odd isn't it?' she asked, but didn't wait for an answer. 'He was a psychologist for nearly thirty years, so maybe it was just some kind of psychology thing, you know?'

'Yes,' Erica replied, though she was doubtful that there would be such an innocent explanation for this. 'Thanks for bringing this to me.'

'Maybe it was just part of his breakdown,' Virginia said, staring into the distance. She looked back at Erica.

'Breakdown, maybe,' Erica said, trying to smile reassuringly. 'Look, just leave this with me. I'm going to show the journal to my partner and see what he makes of it, don't worry about it,' she said, 'and I'm sorry for your loss–'

'Not my loss, anymore.' Virginia smiled sadly.

'Well, you know, the kids. And all this.' Erica gestured to the journal before slipping it into the evidence bag and removing the green gloves. 'Thanks for bringing it in, you did the right thing.' Erica led Virginia back down the long corridor to reception and escorted her out of the front door. 'Bye,' Erica said. 'I'll be in touch.' She watched Virginia walk away up the busy street until she disappeared into the crowd of pedestrians on their lunch breaks.

Oranges

Katyana Rocker-Cook

(A novel extract)

Monday 22nd February 2013

Caroline did her best to pay attention to what her sister Melanie was saying as she steered the trolley towards the fruit aisle. The tinny supermarket music and fluorescent lights were starting to bring the strain of an impending migraine, and Caroline knew she didn't have long to get home before it came in full force. The weekly food shop had always been an issue for Caroline; there was never quite enough room between the shelves for the number of trolleys trying to get past, and for some reason there always seemed to be an impossibly large crowd by the milk, which of course had to be the smallest shelf. And now the trolley was almost full.

'Thanks for watching the kids last night, Caz, me and Darren really appreciate it.'

Caroline hated that her sister called her Caz, but it was a habit she'd had since they were children, and she didn't have the heart to tell her to stop now.

'Don't worry about it, my pleasure,' she said. 'Violet said the funniest thing last night, she…'

Melanie sighed, and turned to her sister with tired eyes.

'Caz, can we please have a conversation that's not about my children? It sounds bad, I know, but since I became a mum all people ever want to talk about is kids. I used to have a life, you know? There must be something interesting about me that isn't my ability to produce two babies for the price of one.'

Caroline laughed and changed the subject to an analysis of last night's dinner. She'd sent them to Parsis, a new Iranian restaurant in town that was on her way to work. Despite how often she'd looked in the window and been tempted by the intriguing smell of coriander and what she thought was star anise, Caroline had never been brave enough to go in. Every afternoon she promised herself that at five thirty, she would reward another long day in the office with something new, something adventurous. A little treat. But every time, she'd get to that green door, and panic. Her stomach would knot over and over itself, and she'd begin pulling at her sleeves with that familiar feeling of yet another attack of anxiety. She thought that if she sent Melanie there first, she could get an idea of what it was like, and maybe even her sister's stamp of approval. With that, she knew she could finally go in. And probably take Melanie with her.

She was so engrossed in her sister's re-telling of the way the waiters set fire to a lump of cheese for a signature course that she didn't notice the impending collision of her trolley with that of the man directly in front of her.

'Oh God, I'm so sorry, how embarrassing.'

Caroline avoided meeting his eyes as she fumbled about rearranging the cans of baked beans that had toppled over in the collision. Eventually she looked up, and was caught by the sparkling chrome hue of his eyes.

'It's ok, happens all the time, right? Looked like a pretty interesting story.'

Caroline felt the blood rush to her cheeks as she turned to her sister, who was doing a very bad job of pretending she needed pears. She looked back at the stranger, whose face held a crooked smile. He was charming, but something about him suggested a kind of control, like everything he said had a purpose. She thought maybe it was his cheekbones; he had something of the classic Bond films about him.

'I'm Jason,' said the man, holding out his hand.

'Caroline.'

'Great to meet you. You need some oranges?'

'Um, yeah sure. Why not.'

*

Thursday 18th June 2015

'Where were you last night?'

Caroline took a deep breath and prepared for another long conversation. Jason stood by the fireplace, his hand resting beside their wedding photograph. He had clearly been waiting for her to come home from work.

'I had to take Melanie's kids to Mum's, you know that.'

'You didn't put it on the calendar.'

'No, but I told you about it in the morning.'

'That's not how we do things.'

Caroline did her best to meet Jason's steely gaze, but found herself unable to look at him without feeling a wash of guilt and shame.

'Jason, Melanie only asked me to help out that morning, there was no point writing it on the calendar. I'm sorry it was so last minute but she's my sister and she needed a hand. You know what it's been like with work for her lately and –'

The table shook as Jason's tight fist slammed down upon it.

'So your sister's problems are more important than mine? I'm your fucking husband, you belong here, at home, with me. I'm sick of you running around town like you have no responsibilities. I ask you to be home, or to at least have the common courtesy to tell me in advance where you're going. This shouldn't come as a surprise to you, Caroline, we've been married for a fucking year and a half. It's not a difficult concept to understand, is it?'

Caroline took a deep breath, and tried to find the best way to calm him down.

The recession had really started to take its toll, and when Jason ultimately lost his position, Caroline knew that he was struggling with the idea of not being able to provide for his wife.

'Babe, I can't imagine how stressed out you must be feeling right now, please try not to take it out on me. I don't always have time to write things on the calendar or let you know where I'm going with much notice. It's been a bit crazy for everyone lately, and I'm doing my best to make life easier.'

Jason's eyes narrowed as he took a step towards her.

'So this is all my fault? Your deadbeat husband lost his job and now you have to provide for him. I get it, you're angry. Angry because we're poor and it's my fault.'

'Jason, come on. I know I have to work a bit more now, but it's hardly as if we're struggling for money; we've got enough put by and on my salary, we can manage easily.'

'That's not the point. I'm the one who should be earning the money, not you. If I had it my way, I'd be the only one working, and you would leave your job. You'd do stuff at home, relax and sort things out here.'

Caroline took her husband's hand and traced her fingers over his knuckles, doing her best to soothe him.

'That's really sweet, babe, but I don't want to leave my job. I think I'd go insane just being at home all the time. I'd just spend the whole day worrying about everything I hadn't managed to get done; at least with work I have a bit of a distraction.'

'Exactly, it's just a distraction from what you're not doing. It would be so much better if you'd lost your job instead of me.'

'I know you don't mean that. Come on, why don't we go out to Gambon's…'

Jason snatched his hand from hers and turned away from her with a jerk. He paced to the fireplace and slammed the heel of his hand into the wall.

'How are we supposed to go to Gambon's? We haven't got any fucking money, you stupid cow.'

Caroline looked at her feet and sighed.

'We have got money; we've got a full salary coming in'

'I don't want your fucking pity money, Caroline. I don't understand why this is so hard for you to understand. Can't you see how humiliating it is for a man to be kept by his wife; people asking after your deadbeat husband who just sits around and –'

'You're not a deadbeat, Jason, you —'

In an instant he was towering over her. Pain and a ringing in her ears as Caroline's head was slammed against the panelled wood behind her. Jason's hand gripped her jaw tightly as his face was inches from hers, his eyes boring furiously into her. His breath was hot on her face, and she did her best to blink back tears and squash the quickly rising panic in her chest.

'You don't fucking interrupt me. You understand? When I'm talking to you, you don't *fucking* interrupt me. It's not respectful, is it? And that's all I'm asking you, Caroline, is to respect me. You can do that, can't you?'

Caroline nodded, staring into those impossibly blue eyes, searching for the man she fell in love with. He was in there somewhere; she knew he was. But she had promised herself that she would never let herself be treated like this, no matter how much her anxiety and love for him made her want to stay.

When he eventually released her with a kiss on the forehead and a nonchalant suggestion that she make her famous Carbonara for dinner, Caroline slipped upstairs, packed an overnight bag, and was out of the front door before Jason had time to process what she was doing. She drove to Melanie's, and convinced her to let her stay the night, at least until she had her thoughts straight.

*

'I just don't understand why he reacted like that. He's never looked at me like that before, like he really wanted to hurt me.'

'Listen, he's a shit for what he did, and you shouldn't let him get away with it, but it could have been a lot worse if you were with a proper scumbag. Jason would never really hurt you, he's crazy about you. He's a passionate guy, and men like that just lose it sometimes. I mean I'd definitely make him suffer a bit for it, but ultimately I wouldn't read too much into it. He's always been far more romantic than Darren's ever been for me.'

Caroline sighed. Melanie had a point, but just because Jason said he loved her, that didn't necessarily mean he would never lose it with her. Tonight was a prime example of that.

'I don't know, Mel, you didn't see the way he was looking at me.'

'It was the heat of the moment though, wasn't it? I mean, maybe you're right, I wasn't there so I can't really say, and of course you're welcome to stay over if you're scared. But I think he's just really struggling with not being able to look after you the way he wants to. I know it's silly, but that's what some men are like, isn't it? I mean, Darren wouldn't give a monkeys if he was the one not working, he'd probably quite enjoy the kept life, but that's because he's a lazy, soft bugger, and that's why I married him. But you married Jason because he was strong, and proud, and wanted to make a fuss over you. I mean, God, do you remember your first date?'

Caroline smiled and nodded. Of course she remembered.

*

Friday 2nd March 2013

'I'm really glad we finally got round to doing this.'

Caroline smiled shyly and looked down at her shoes. Something about the way Jason held her hand, firm and with the odd reassuring squeeze, made her feel safer than she had felt for a long time.

'Me too,' she said, 'And I can't wait to try that mushroom soufflé you told me about.'

'Oh, it's incredible, you're going to love it. I've been coming here for years, it's such a wonderful find.'

Caroline had to hand it to him, he had great taste in restaurants. It was clear he was a regular customer; he knew each of the waiters personally and they all went out of their way to make sure everything was exactly as he requested, right down to the distance between the meat and vegetable aspects of his meal. During dessert, he reached across the table and took her hand in his.

'Can I just say, you have the most exquisite hair. It's really quite a beautiful colour.'

Caroline blushed and looked down again, unsure how to respond. She looked up to see Jason smiling at her, clearly amused by her embarrassment.

'Thank you,' she said, 'that's really sweet of you to say.'

*

Thursday 18th June 2015

Caroline distracted herself from thoughts about her fight with Jason as she helped Melanie put the kids to bed, and clear up after dinner. It was gone ten when there was that distinctive knock at the door; one followed by a pause, then three in quick succession. Caroline hesitated for a moment, before slowly approaching the door and opening to find Jason standing before her.

'Babe, I'm sorry. Please don't do this.'

'Jason, I can't talk right now, I'm really busy with –'

'I love you Caroline, I don't work without you. Please.'

It wasn't unusual for Jason to come out with lines like that, but this was the first time he'd said it whilst armed with a bowl of fruit and Caroline's favourite flowers.

'I brought you some oranges, babe. Like when we first met, you remember? I thought it would make you laugh. Plus, we're running low at home so I thought you know, two birds and all that.'

Caroline heard Melanie laugh from the living room, clearly eavesdropping. She turned and saw her smiling knowingly, gesturing for her to go forward and accept her husband's charmingly strange apology. She found herself smiling too, and then she was back in his arms, tightly wrapped where she promised she always would be.

'That,' she began, 'Is completely insane.'

*

Tuesday 4th January 2017

Two years passed, and Caroline was content with the two more years of marriage that came with it. Life with Jason was secure, straightforward.

He had a way of planning the perfect evenings: every event from her birthday to Christmas and Valentine's Day were spent at Gambon's; the restaurant where they'd had their first date. A week before their anniversary, Caroline decided it was his turn to be spoiled, so following Melanie's recommendation she booked a window table at the Iranian place and bought him a set of interlinking heart cufflinks. She got off work early, and had a bottle of 1996 Barolo breathing on the living room table ready for Jason's return. She smoothed the skirt of her dress as she heard his car pull onto the drive, smiling to herself as she thought about the evening ahead. Jason entered the room, arms brimming with a bouquet of white roses.

'Hey, how was work? I've been looking forward to dinner with you all day.'

Since Jason had got back on his feet with a higher paying job and longer hours, he'd convinced Caroline to leave her job after all, and prepare the house for the possibility of a family. It didn't take much persuasion; these days Caroline was happy to do anything to make Jason happy. He was doting, funny, and charismatic when he was in a good mood. He was always the biggest hit at her parents' summer barbecues and dinner parties, gliding through business talks with Caroline's father, and effortlessly charming her mother with compliments about the house, the food, her hair. It was clear to Caroline that she had made the right choice in marrying him, and for once she felt like she had something she could be proud of. She knew that Jason was far better looking than she could ordinarily have hoped to achieve, and he certainly got along better with her family than any of her previous boyfriends.

Jason smiled as he set the roses on the table and examined the wine.

'Me too. I've been thinking about that mushroom soufflé all afternoon.'

'Oh honey, I actually booked a table at that Iranian place I sent Melanie and Jack to that time. I've been wanting to go for ages.'

Jason's brows twitched together as annoyance flickered across his face. He took a deep breath and smiled down at his eager wife.

'But we always go to Gambon's. It's our restaurant.'

'I know, babe, but this place is so romantic and Melanie said the food is incredible. I just thought it would be nice to have a change, and you know, Melanie told me the best story about what they do with the cheese…'

Jason firmly placed his hands upon his wife's shoulders and gritted his teeth, his breath slow and controlled.

'Caroline, I thought I'd made it clear before that I don't want you changing the way we do things. We've always gone to Gambon's, and we will continue to do so for as long as you are married to me. Now we can still have a lovely evening, I'll phone Gambon's and get this sorted out. Why don't you go and put on the dress I got you for your birthday, I love how that looks.'

He kissed her head and poured a glass of the Barolo. Caroline hesitated, unsure how to handle the situation. She didn't want to upset Jason, but she was starting to worry that the damage had already been done. She pulled at the sleeve of her cardigan, the dark bruise on her forearm catching the corner of her eye. She didn't want to risk another outburst, but this was different. Jason got angry when she changed little things about the house, or if she wasn't home when she was supposed to be. But this was a nice gesture, surely he'd see that? She decided to continue trying to persuade him; she had to make some decisions after all. She moved over to the table, gently taking Jason's hand and running her fingers over his knuckles.

'I know you like to go to Gambon's,' she began, 'but I thought it would be nice to do something a bit different. You always plan these wonderful evenings and I wanted to do the same for you. And it's not as if I'm taking you somewhere completely random; we know this place is popular and Melanie's been back hundreds of times, she loves it there.'

The sound of glass hitting hardwood flooring cut her words short, as Jason took a step towards her, his feet crunching the shattered wine bottle underfoot. She felt very aware of his eyes upon her, and humiliated that she couldn't bring herself to meet them. She slowly retreated back, though she knew that trying to get away from him would be futile. Her eyes flicked down to the floor, which was beginning to resemble a crime scene as Jason's advance was tracked by red prints.

'I don't quite know how to deal with you at the moment, Caroline. It's strange, because it seems to me that you're determined to make this a miserable affair. I have told you time and again that I couldn't give two fucks about what your sister tells you, or any fancy new ideas you get about what we're going to do in our relationship. Now I don't know what you're trying to pull here, but I suggest you reconsider before you turn this night into something quite unfortunate.'

Caroline took a deep breath, before finally meeting her husband's eyes with an apologetic smile. A part of her had always known that changing their plans would be a risk, and there was no point trying to persuade him now. Her heart beat violently against her chest, and she concentrated on controlling her breathing and appearing calm, unafraid. It only upset him more when she got scared. A nice evening, that's all she wanted.

'You're right. I'm sorry, babe, really. I wasn't trying to upset you, I just thought it would be nice to have a change, but it was a stupid idea and you're completely right. I'll go and change and we can go to Gambon's like you said.'

Jason turned and walked away from his wife, flexing his fingers and making his way to the phone on the coffee table.

'Before you change,' he said, dialling the number for Gambon's, 'will you clean up this mess. I will sort out a table and try to salvage what's left of our evening.'

This extract is taken from Chapter One of a novella, Oranges:

Oranges follows the marriage of Caroline and Jason over a ten-year period. As Caroline begins to understand the sort of man she has married in Jason, she finds herself cut off from those she loves, and must choose between pursuing happiness elsewhere, or standing by the man she once fell in love with.

Two in the Bush

Christian Deery

(A short story)

A foppish-looking man entered the fray. 'Sir, Ranger Williams has made an arrest. If you could please come and meet him at the clock tower, just as soon as you've finished your…'. The man looked closer at the Mayor's breakfast. 'Asparagus?'

The bespectacled mayor looked up from his Playboy magazine and through a mouthful of food said, 'Okay, that will be all, Mr. A Foppish Looking Man.' The Mayor removed his 3D glasses, and at once set off for the clock tower.

He was met by Ranger Rob Williams. Rob's head was longer than the average head, similar to those sausage-shaped balloons that clowns or failed magicians manipulate into 'animals'. He wore a homemade uniform of sewn-together pieces of various paintball outfits. The predominant colour was red camouflage, the most useless of all camouflage. Rob regarded his two captives with a snarl.

'Please keep the snarling to a minimum, Mr Williams, it is more befitting of a dog with Snarling Syndrome,' said the Mayor. 'You must be Paul?' the Mayor looked to a sallow-faced man who wore a nametag that said 'Paul'.

'Nah, my name's Julian. Julian Sallowface.'

The Mayor addressed the female. 'And who might you be, my dear?'

'I'm his wife, Pam, Frying Pam,' said the female companion, who had a face that, if one had to compare to a household appliance, resembled a nine-inch frying pan.

The Mayor took Rob to one side briefly and said, 'What's the deal here, Rob? I was reading a lovely article about how, in America, white privileged males can basically get away with rape. Especially if they're promising athletes. A fantastic read.'

'Well Mr Mayor, I'm just going to ignore that comment, as it seems like something perhaps satirical? Or political? I am poor so therefore I don't understand satire or politics. I just eat crisps and watch television. Preferably programmes where I can watch other people actually watching telly. That's the kind of stuff I'm interested in.'

'I'm sorry, Rob, I don't recall asking for any kind of back story about you. You're superfluous. Now perform your duty of relaying these events, and then leave in some sort of humorous way at a later point.'

'Why thank you Mayor, I've never been called 'super' before. Anyway, let me start from the beginning, I was performing my usual duty of following people around the town centre for no reason, when...' said Rob.

'Please, begin in medias res, it makes for a much better tale.'

'...so after that hilarious turn of events, I arrested them.'

'Well, what an unlikely tale of two people having sex in a bush. How old might you be, Julian?' asked the Mayor.

'I might be fifty-one or fifty-two, not sure.'

'Pam, do you admit to the crime you have been accused of?' asked the Mayor.

'If falling in love with a shoplifter and having sex with him in a bush near a playground is a crime, then yes, sue me.'

'Well, falling in love with a shoplifter certainly carries a hefty penalty around these parts. What is your occupation, Julian?'

'I'm a graduate of alcoholism, apprentice shoplifter. I've also got a Masters degree in Hair and Philosophy.'

'What exactly were you doing in the bush?' The Mayor directed this question toward Pam and put on his 3D glasses.

The pair looked to each other for moral support, but neither answered.

'It was her fault, Your Majesty. See, I have an incredible weakness for oversized waistcoats. It's my Kryptonite. It makes me almost as stiff as an erect penis. You could say it's my Dicktonite.'

The Mayor hadn't noticed the mauve waistcoat that clung to Pam, the way a slice of bacon might cling to a cocktail sausage (if one were preparing particularly unattractive looking pigs in blankets).

'Well, we are all partial to a waistcoat, Julian, and Kryptonite is certainly a fine brand, but this has really got you in a pickle.'

'This isn't a pickle, it's a pair of trousers,' said Julian.

'Oh, do forgive me. You are however, in a bit of a quandary, should I say?'

Julian was on the verge of tears.

'Please step away from that verge, Julian. It's a dangerous drop there,' said the Mayor.

Julian took a step back and turned to face his wife. 'Why have you done this to us, you and your damn waistcoats? And now we have been arrested, don't you realise?'

Frying Pam's face now looked as though it had been greased with 1 calorie cooking spray, for she was sweating profusely. 'I understand very well what's happening here. This ludicrous turn of events has shamed us Julian, I only hope that the kind Mayor will spare us the embarrassment of having to face the courts.' Pam contorted her face in a way which was clearly supposed to seduce the Mayor into feeling sorry for her, but this only served to make her resemble a saucepan.

Pam then performed a three-sixty degree turn, as though she was on a catwalk, and addressed the Mayor. 'Years ago, back when Julian was a chief executive alcoholic, I met him outside the pub. He wooed me with dry roasted peanuts. He'd just won three pounds on a scratch card, and offered to buy me a drink of my choice. The choice was between water and sparkling water. I wanted to impress him so I went for the sparkling stuff to show that I knew what it was like to live on the right side of the tracks. We all know what atrocities occur on the left side of the tracks. In those days, Julian was not as hideously unattractive as he is now, in fact he looked like a rather pleasant dry roasted peanut. We spent all evening together, and agreed to meet for a second date later that week. That's when we went to Caldecott Park.'

Rob, the town ranger, who had remained silent and motionless since his last contribution to the conversation, acknowledged this with a grunt. Caldecott Park was one of his prime hunting grounds for following innocent shoppers. There was no real need for Rob to be stood around anymore. His snorts were neither warranted or pleasant.

The Mayor turned to him and said, 'Rob, I heard a rumour there was a particularly disruptive pigeon causing some trouble around Asda. Apparently, he's been giving it all that.'

This was a phrase Rob knew well, and usually meant one of two things: A. The pigeon had stolen some form of carbohydrate from a fat woman or B. He was a suspected terrorist. Rob pulled out a device that said, 'Pigeon Taser 3000'. 'I'll go and blast him with my new Pigeon Taser Five Thousand.' And with that blatant lie, he took his mole-infested face towards Asda.

'Do forgive Rob, he has a habit of making a mountain out of a moleface.'

Pam and Julian burst into fits of laughter.

'Could you guys keep those fits of laughter to mere titters?' asked the Mayor.

'Ha! It was your titters that got us into this mess, Pam,' said Julian.

Frying Pam's face turned red as though someone had just turned up the hob.

The Mayor felt repulsed for the first time today. Her 'titters' looked like sagging teabags through her waistcoat. The Mayor imagined that they were dirty and misshapen. 'So, Miss Pam, you were saying…'

'Yeah so, for our second date we went to Caldecott Park. The day was full of wonder and butterflies. Flutterbies I used to call them as a kid. I don't know if they kept a farm around here or something but they seemed to be everywhere. There was a sweet moment when a black and gold butterfly landed on Julian's nose. I brushed it off, gently like a stray eyelash. It was the first time we had touched.' Pam turned and looked at Julian, who nodded in agreement. If one had to compare Julian to any piss-infested bar snack he really did look like a dry roasted peanut as Pam had suggested but one who had a peanut allergy and was allergic to his own face.

'I always called Julian 'My Butterfly' after that.' Pam continued. 'Anyway, we strolled through the park hand in hand. Birds greeted us with their song. Julian was convinced that a chaffinch was singing Coldplay to us. I said, 'That's ridiculous Julian. That's clearly a Blue-tit.'
'Ha! It was your blue tits that got us into this mess in the first place, Pam,' said Julian.

'They're not blue, they're green.'

'Whatever, they were blue when I spilt my WKD onto them that time.'

'I'm trying to tell Our Royal Highness a story here, Julian. So, we had a go on the swings, the slide, and even those little springy animals, then at last we arrived at a bush next to a bench; this thorn bush seemed an obvious place to sit. But that wasn't the only bush Julian was interested in, though it did contain significantly less wildlife than my own.'

Julian interjected, 'So we were in this bush and you'll never believe it. A butterfly lands right between Pam's legs. And, of course, I do the gentlemanly thing of grabbing at it, except my hand cramps up, and gets stuck there. Silly old Pam thought I was trying to feel her up.'

'We are not ones to talk about our private lives so let's just say we made love,' Pam finished.

Night soon hit. A haunting light shone from the clock tower above them, which read the incorrect time. The Mayor gestured to a nearby bench and the three took a seat together.

Pam continued, 'We were married within the year. A beautiful ceremony. The Salvation Army did us a discount. They did us a buffet and everything. Crisps, sandwiches, crisps… you name it!'

'Trifle?' asked the Mayor reluctantly.

'No, but we had sandwiches and crisps.'

Julian perked up, 'Oh I love crisps, me. And peanuts.'

'And sandwiches, Julian?' asked Pam.

'Oh yeah. I love a good sandwich. Crisp sandwiches are my favourite.'

'I quite like trifle myself,' said the Mayor.

'This conversation is becoming a bit trifling,' said Julian. No one laughed.

'So yes, the marriage. We had our rough patches. The time we gave each other crabs. We both had rough patches that week.'

'Have you told him about the crisps yet?' asked Julian.

'Yes, you ignoramus. But seriously, Mayor. There were some tough times but we got through them, you know like how a caterpillar fights its way out of a cocoon. It's a struggle you know, but worth it in the end.'

'Except, I've been a caterpillar for too long. I'm an old caterpillar still clawing my way out of that cocoon. And today I saw my chance. The chance to spread my wings. So, this morning, I got up and went straight out to buy this waistcoat, came back, woke Julian and off we set to the park. All the old feelings came back. I felt reinvigorated.'

'It was only when Julian came across the bush that the sex was complete, sperm everywhere.'

'Then your mate Rob nicked us,' piped Julian, 'I hadn't even put my cock away before he pulled that pigeon taser on us. Although he referred to it as a 'Cock Taser 6000' at the time and threatened to 'taser' my 'willy' into 'next week', and then, get this, 'back again!' You can imagine, the whole ordeal was quite frightening. I'm quite poor so I probably shouldn't be allowed an opinion on this but I don't think that guy should be walking the streets if I'm honest.'

Pam then took the reins, 'Look, Mr Mayor, I am getting old. We were just trying to rekindle that old youthful flame and got carried away.' She then let go of Julian's reins.

The Mayor rose. That was his name, Mayor Rose. He remained seated, and then rose. 'I wouldn't dream of punishing you after that wonderful tale. It has almost brought a tear to my eye. Please, go on and enjoy your evening.'

The couple said their goodbyes. Once out of sight of the Mayor, who sat contemplating the tale he had been told, they walked into a sandwich shop that specialized in crisp sandwiches, where the bread was crisps and the filling was also crisps.

Julian turned to Pam and said, 'All that for a bloody shag!'

Poetry

Christian Deery

Yarn from the Barn

Oi wai'ed in the barn for 'er tha' noit.
Oi was so exoi'ed, I was shakin'.
Don't know w'a' oi was anticipa'in'.
Jus' a smale fumble under the moonloit?
Walkin' 'er down the oisle in milky woit?
There she came through the gai'. Me quakin'
In me wellies, and 'er standin' uproit.
'er long, slim brown legs shinin' like a spring
bu"ercup. And eyes clear loike th' purest
dymond. She woon't share 'er precious carats
with anyone else. Oi feel so grateful.
As she approaches, oi see she's well dressed
In 'er favourite pink hooves and red beret
O'er 'er mane. This noit will be fateful.

Small Town Boy

Twenty-two minutes since I turned thirty.
It's not just my heart that's broken.
It's the whole fucking system.

I write smiles with a stolen pencil.
I speak deeply but draw shallow breaths.
I paint pleasantries upon people,
With a dishonest tongue.
My history is written in hazy graffiti.

Holding my breath to survive.
I just want someone to cry with.
But the tears won't come.

Bizarre Blurbs. An ode to 'Goosebumps'

1. Rolf is in love with shit instruments and crap art. But the crap art only has eyes for Lawrence Sheriff, an ex-butcher with a penchant for vegetarianism. How can a fat Australian compete with such a rival? He concocts a bold plan to win the art's love, involving some beard combs and a whole army of loyal Oompa Loompas. Will Rolf's worthless existence in the entertainment industry be rewarded? And what is to become of the two little boys with two wooden heads that he keeps in his cage?

2. Jeremy has won an oversized hand and is now on his way to 'grab' it. But the British transport system has gone wrong, whisking Jez and John Virgo into orbit and a hysterically dangerous adventure. *The classic sequel to 'Beadle's About' and the prequel to the unforgettable 'Beadle's Dead'*

3. Quentin's Grandmother has the *dirtiest* house in the *world*...so dirty even those bastards Kim and Aggie wouldn't enter. But Quent, a pathetically awful illustrator decides she needs to be taught a lesson. He concocts a wicked plan to short-circuit her stairlift while a packet of Werther's Originals hangs just out of reach. He will watch the plan unfold until her Highland blanket dissolves from her own urine. In fact, now he thinks about it, the blanket is one step too far. He might as well just leave her until she turns into a hessian rucksack, as is her custom.

4. Caroline is a habitually *boring freak,* but her parents think she is *fun.* When one day Caz is attacked by Phil and Grant following an argument about the futility of Essex, she discovers she has a remarkable power to prove her parents *wrong.* This captivating story is complemented by songs by the Man with the Iron Voice.

5. It's not much fun being made out of snow. When Jack and Frost stumble across the ice-making machine, the place is suddenly a blizzard. There are White Fangs and Lassies the size of *dogs* everywhere. Will the two snowmen ever replace their carrots with substantial penises?

Pre-Nuptial

'You broke my heart.
Now I want my kidney back.'

'You can have it back but I want half.'

The Cause of Many Wars

Arms stretched out like the star of Israel
Bullets of rain pelting bowed head
They shoot to the ground
Hands soaked in blood
Can't wash away
Hordes brave the weather
In formation
They kneel to pray

The Confession of Hezekiah J Holt

Kurt Shead

(A short story)

Saturday, December 29th, the Year of Our Lord 1819, London, England

Herein is written a true account and confession of Hezekiah J. Holt, for those who seek knowledge beyond the grave.

My name is Hezekiah Jaron Holt, son of Abraham and Jessica. I sit confined in London's Tower; the door of my cell is locked. Candlelight is my only companion, and the moon is cradled betwixt the bars of my window, like a strand of wheat. I have done murder, and I am to hang at dawn. This document, for any soul who may deign to read it, stands as mine own explanation of motive; it is, I move to emphasise, no defence of my actions. The law of this land writes murder as capital; my guilt is not in question, only the reason as to its engorgement. It is, I think, fathomable.

But then, all madmen who speak with God believe that their conversations stand to reason. Perhaps I am such. It is not then the man who guards outside my cell who is my gaoler, but He that sits enthroned above, and his keys are the keys to the Kingdom. If you believe in such fancies.

On my father's side, I am born from a long military history. We may not have been worthy enough to be of distinction, but we have performed our patriotic duty with quiet diligence. My grandfather served in the War of the Spanish Succession, fighting at Saragossa; his son served as a lieutenant under Abercrombie at Carillon against the French. He lost a hand for his involvement. Therefore, it is probable my father assumed my life would follow a similar path. However, I have always been possessed of a great disdain for authority; my destined career was pocked with disaster from the first, doomed to fail. I shot a pig one night in my company's mess hall after drinking too much. I was disciplined; in retaliation, I defecated in my commander's chamber, and proceeded to abandon my post. A warrant was issued for my arrest; my father was ashamed, and it was only his love for my mother and her corresponding pleas that convinced him not to aid in my recapture. I thank him for that much, at least.

I escaped England by joining a ship's crew as a lowly deckhand; my captain was Augustus Tirell, a man who, on paper, was a merchant of spices, silks and other exotic wares found only in the farthest corners of the globe. He was an accomplished sailor, but docks are full of whispers, and they yielded more than attestation to a simple trading business. His ship's name, I should mention, was *Sorrow*.

You have, perhaps, heard the name before today? For years, we sailed across the Atlantic, the Mediterranean, the North Sea; wherever you could hear the crashing of waves, *Sorrow* sowed its seeds. Yes, I confess, I partook in the pirate's lot. I am descended from a military pedigree, and the inherent lawlessness of a pirate's life appealed to my unfulfilled wildness. It was here I began to excel; I led from the front, blood often on my blade, and so earned the respect of the savage men that surrounded me. I climbed through the ranks, until I stood at Gus's right hand. But always I strived to remain nameless; Gus's reputation eclipsed mine utterly, and that is how I preferred it.

I do not know what I had planned to do after my career of blood and infamy. I was richer than a prince; perhaps I would sail west and live out my days in warmth and prosperity. I even entertained the thought of returning to England; I would see my family again, and perhaps my father would be proud; not of my occupation, but of my ability. I realise now, however, that it was only ever a fantasy in my mind; I do not think I would have ever returned to my native land, unless I was forced to do so.

It is interesting how Fate works, is it not? For events were about to conspire that, indeed, forced me back to the place of my birth.

We had put in at Port Royal when I received the message, handed to me by a street urchin without a word; it bore a mysterious waxen seal, the device of which I could not identify. It had no signature; how could I be certain of its authenticity? Any man with his faculties intact would have been suspicious; a bolder man would simply throw such cryptic conspiracy to the fire. Yet, in its defence, the message was laden with accuracy; my father was dead, it told me. My mother had been remarried these past five years, and now she herself was ill, fatally. Whomever the author was, he seemed greatly informed on my family's most private affairs.

But, however accurate the letter's content might have been (or might not have been, should that proved to be the case) it was not that which convinced me of its truth. I am not a God-fearing man, and nor do I possess any inclination towards the existence of the supernatural. Yet I cannot explain the reason my blood ran cold, or why I sensed the sword of Damocles poised above me.

There was much more to that letter that I have hitherto left unspoken; I assure you that I shall reveal all before the closing of this statement. Suffice it to say that my icy veins thawed, then rose to boil inside me like a sickness on my journey back to London.

I stole away in the middle of the night. I said not a word to Gus about my abrupt departure. I abandoned him, quite simply, after more than a decade of brotherhood. I still feel the guilt of it to this day. He is dead now, most likely; whether by the ravages of time or the hangman's noose, it makes no difference. I booked passage home on an ancient galley named *The Bondsman*. You might well guess at its vocation; indeed, the British had abolished the slave trade in 1807. Still, I was aboard a slave ship, and it had a cargo of flesh. But you did not need to view the poor souls to know they were below, crammed like meat into the hold; stand a mile downwind and the ship's stench betrayed its purpose well enough. I will not describe the unnumbered horrors I witnessed on that hellish voyage. Men became beasts, blood replaced the blueness of the salt ocean, and my soul fell to rot until I could peel it away like so many strips of hide. Murder came soundly into my hands ever after.

I get ahead of my own chronology. The eastern Luomoko tribe of the Dark Continent has a saying; it has no direct translation into English. But, as far as I can make it, it means "you must swallow the beast whole to eat."

Here we are brought into closer proximity with more recent events. The man I willingly killed went beneath the alias of one Elmo Baymen; few men knew his true name. Luckily for me, the name of Holt still carries some weight; his name was, I discovered after some investigation, Edward Richard Booke, a man of infamy in London's lower society; he was a confidence man, some say a talented one. The story goes that he began his career as a conspicuous mountebank in Devil's Acre, selling vials of urine mixed with whale's oil as a wondrous health tonic. When this enterprise failed to yield profit, Booke honed his duplicity upon individuals; his favoured prey, the wives or daughters of rich merchants. My Mother was such a woman. Too kind, too trusting, and far, far too good for this sorry world. The more emotionally astute amongst you may begin to guess at my reason for coming home; perhaps you also begin to understand why Booke needed to die swiftly. And painfully.

He was known to frequent Marley's tavern on Cork Lane; he was one of their more exuberant patrons, buying liquor for the regular customers in return for their indiscretion. Men that reside at the centre of their own importance are not difficult to find. I found him holding court at Marley's one cold evening in November. He was certainly a gregarious figure, larger than life, one could say. I fancied that he merely surfeited upon his own delusions; an occupational hazard of such men.

Forgive me. My thoughts wander like errant pilgrims, and the hand can but follow. I shall endeavour to remain true to course.

Booke was evidently a man who had never struggled to capture an audience. With all humility, I can assure you that I am possessed of something similar. In the North Americas, the redskin peoples venerate their elders to nothing we could hope to equal in our country of Christian pretensions. There was one woman, of the Chowanoc tribe, who was respected by her entire community, and held in awe even by the Europeans who settled close to them on the opposing side of the river. They said she was a shaman, an ancient mystic that drank blood and talked to the animal dead. She cackled at me when I relayed these suspicions. Her people called her Flower Mother; she was a healer, a chieftainess. She spoke softly, and her people listened. She taught me how to weave a story, how to close mouths and open ears.

It worked well on Booke. I was quiet and intense, and I spoke of splendid things. Booke was easily sold. I supplied him with drink upon drink, adding a little something of my own to his tincture when he staggered out of the tavern for temporary relief. Flower Mother was a healer to her tribe, yes, and knew her remedies well; she could brew potions to make a maiden fertile, and others to make the men potent. She had mixtures that would steal away pain behind the eyes, or steady a shaking hand. There was another, a bitter leaf that, when crushed to a powder, could be stirred into food or drink with little taste. A pinch could make a grown man drowsy, a spoonful might send him into a peaceful sleep. Three spoons might stop his heart. I gave Booke just enough to make him submissive to my intentions.

I brought Booke to my family's estate on Lower Mount Street. The door was locked, and I had no key. When you are as travelled as I, you learn that one lock is much like another. I was once in the company of a man reputed to be the best thief on the Indian Continent. He was a diminutive fellow; slight, and quick-fingered. He told me a story of how he had stolen a pair of golden earrings right from the ears of a Mughal emperor. As if in proof, he brushed the hair back from his left ear; there was the earring, glinting, shaped into a tiger's head. He claimed to have given the other away; one was more than enough, he said. Luckily, I had no such challenge; the lock fell easily to my hands, as many had over the years.

I had long decided on what form my revenge would take, and had made my preparations. I brought thick ropes with me for the task, so as to bind him to a chair whilst my plan unfurled. I had a cloth to gag him, and an assortment of instruments to orchestrate his demise.

As a martial man, the people of the cold North fascinate me. Theirs is a culture of warriors; the women can be just as ferocious as their men, sometimes more so. They have pagan blood running in their veins, ancient as seawater. Their ancestors fought with axes and rounded shields, putting civilisations to the torch and singing songs as they died and walked from this world to feast in eternal golden halls.

A silly belief, and yet these folk cling to their fabled history as a wolf covets the kill. I once met a man who claimed to be a descendent of the last of the Jomsvikings. He was an old man, but strong and built like the trunk of an oak. Hair rested upon his brows like a crown of snow, and his eyes – a startling shade of blue – brought sapphires to mind. He told me that for a man to become a Jomsviking, he must undergo a rite of initiation. The man must drink a concoction of stewed roots mixed with a dangerous spice; only having done this would the man be able to traverse worlds and do battle with the gods. Those that succeeded were inducted into the Jomsviking order; those that failed lost their minds, doomed to die and die again in unending battle.

It is with such a potion I began to have my way with Booke. He was mellowed enough to drink of it. His countenance shifted at once; his eyes popped wide from their sockets, and the veins on his neck stood out like the whips of slavers. Strings of pale froth dripped from the corners of his mouth as his face stretched into a static rictus of agony. What twisted visions danced before his eyes? A place where his whores turned to wolves and gold made the shell of his skin run molten. I know now why some men describe pain as exquisite.

My approach then took on a more practical aspect. I have always had an affinity with knives; I could bring down a bird with a throwing knife as surely as another man might use a rifle. Gus used to jest that I could join the circus when I had done away with the pirate's life. There is a certain blade I insisted on incorporating into my revenge; it has a hooked end, and it is thin and delicate enough to slice between layers of skin. The Kings of Assyria used to flay insubordinate nobles and are said to have hanged their skins from the columns within the city, as a warning to others who might make their discontent known. I do not know if this story is grounded in truth; nonetheless, it is from here that I took my precedent. I started small; fingers, toes. I left Booke for long periods to maximise his suffering, and kept each piece of flayed skin as a memento.

I will not go into any more overt details; I run the risk of indulging myself. I took a hammer to his knees; I cut off his ears. I put out his eyes and sewed his mouth shut so that he might never speak another lie. By the end, I was awash in blood, all of it his.

Booke survived his ordeal fairly admirably. By the end of the third day, he ceased to struggle. By the morning of the fifth he was dead. I collected his remains into sacks and threw them into the Thames. One sack washed ashore on the South Bank hours later; it contained Booke's right foot, the lower part of his torso, and his head. The head was, admittedly, my undoing. I was not quiet in my investigations, nor was I delicate in my hospitality towards this man. My trail was easy to follow, just like the blood. And just like the screams.

One might say that it was my desire to be discovered, or that I was careless in its regard to the least. I surrendered myself up to the proper authorities without issue or complaint. I am guilty, yes. But I am not sorry. Now, I await justice.

It is the question of justice that pushes me to document this statement in writing. I am thirty-two years of age, but my life draws to its final sunset. I am not proud of my savagery; a normal man must beat down the monster which lurks in his soul.

Yet, I ask you; who protected my mother from the monster within Booke? He left her to die, destitute and alone. He stole her love for years, and left her with nothing. He took her home for his debts, and continued to live on as before, unabashed, and utterly without shame. What was I to do? My father is dead; the law did nothing. I was all that was left, and I showed him the justice of the grave.

I hear footsteps outside my cell. Is it time already? The cold half-light of dawn enters through my window, and my doom approaches.

I wish you a full life, and luck against your own monsters.

— *Hezekiah Holt.*

Poetry

Kurt Shead

Forest Man

The Forest is your garden, and in your eyes
I see your heart

The day comes, bruised and tear-stricken
You wipe away its fears, warm water, and soap
Your breath smells like mint
The stars drowse, dimming
They fall; you catch them in a silken bag
Pulling the drawstring
Your hands feel like the Earth
The sun comes, and smiles at you
You smile back; you wave
Your eyes are filled with sky

One boot, then two
Over-big, both wreathed in yesterday's mud
Mittens, a scarf to keep out the cold
And a pointed hat; patched, collapsed, melted
Your coat? A woven thing; leaves, stitched to hides
Green, and living, embroidered with birdsong and moonwish
A carven staff. You may as well complete my picture

Moonshine

Your soles creak across the floorboards
Down the stairs, out the door
You close it behind you with a soft *schnick*
All is quiet; the fog hampers, a scent of clouds
You pass through, following the path
When it rains, the path turns to milk
Laughing as it runs about your feet

Humming, baritone, tuneless, you enter the Forest
You are home

You touch the tree bark; it breathes
Why didn't you tell me – what is its name?
No, I'm wrong. You told me all
I just had not the ears to listen

I am listening now

Tell me the names of colours, of smells
Tell me what they're called, or what you call them by
Oak is greatness; Aspen is groaning
Hawthorne dares to hope; Willow is swept weeping
Fir, Elder, Elm; brothers, your children
Hemlock, flaxweed, dragonlance, chrysanthemum
Nightshade, aconite, lavender, and thyme
How many of those did you make up?
It does not matter. It has never mattered to me
You grin, eyes greener than our Forest

Now nut, berry, whortle and cone
An offering of scattered bounty
You bend, and pluck from the ground, to eat

Thankful for your handful of mud
You separate the earth worm, and return him where he belongs
You walk on, into the heart of the Forest. Into mine

You have your favourite place; a pool, black as night
Neath the shade of the trees
You stare into it, you stare back, emeralds from the depths
You recline, removing your boots
You paddle your feet in the water, stopping time for me
You are happy; this is your place
But it cannot be mine

A day came when I left our Forest
It was living then, and green with your life
But I forgot the names of leaves
Whilst you slumbered beneath the dreams of trees
Until you say my name, the last name you have remembered

The leaves have turned from green to brown
You come to the Forest later each day
Your eyes sparkle still, but they are small
And they look further away, to something I cannot see
Many times, you lose yourself in our Forest
Your feet tread the path to the pool
You paddle your feet in the water, shoes on still
You smile, and you are happy; you don't know why

And one day came when I came to the pool
You were not there to meet me
All the trees had laid down their burden of leaves
They are old now, and black. It is raining
I walk away

Moonshine

I come to your house
There is no light
The door swings in on its own accord, haunted
I drag myself up the steps to where you used to sleep
I cannot walk

You lie on your bed, small
Your lips are slightly blue
Your face is calm, at peace
Upon your pyre of woven dreams

Your heart has ceased to beat
You are back in the Forest, Forest Man!
You are in the very heart of our Forest, and in mine
And there you will always be.

Confessions of an English Gentleman

Charlotte Symons

(A novel extract)

Chapter 1

The man was dressed entirely in black. His breeches were black, his coat was black and so was the cravat at his neck. Black silk stockings clothed his legs and his face was covered by a black mask. The only relief came from the silver threadwork which dusted his coat like stars in a winter sky. In the midst of the ballroom, surrounded by silks of many colours, the starkness of his dress set him apart.

Yet it was more than that. It was the man himself, the manner in which his slim figure weaved its way through the brightly-coloured throng, like a figure of death from a medieval mystery play. Unlike the other guests, clustered in huddles, he moved alone, slipping between and around those assembled as though bound on a mission all his own. It is hard to convey to you the effect he had on me – why should a man moving across a ballroom be something I could hardly tear my eyes from? And yet I freely admit I was magnetised.

I studied those nearby, expecting to see a similar fascination to my own. Yet as I watched, I began to observe something odd. It was as if no-one else noticed him. Watching his dancing path across the ballroom, I saw that it was always him, the man in black, who stepped aside in order to let others pass and yet, in so doing, somehow lost none of the authority and presence that so drew me to him.

I crossed to where Henry stood nursing a glass of wine. Determined to enter fully into the spirit of things, Henry had purchased a Harlequin outfit for the evening. Earlier, when we were readying ourselves in our lodgings, he had been delighted with the effect but now, to judge by his bashful manner, his confidence had somewhat wilted.

On seeing me, he rallied. 'You haven't got a drink, Charles. That won't do – can't go to a ball and not have a drink.'

'In a minute. Henry, do you see that man? There, in the black, by that woman in yellow.' I pointed.

Henry gazed across the room in the direction indicated by my outstretched finger. 'I wouldn't call it yellow – not really. More of a gold, or even a light chestnut. Matter of fact, my brother had a horse almost the exact same colour once. Pretty little filly. White socks. Jumped like you wouldn't believe. Silly fool was heartbroken when he lost her at cards.'

'Not that woman, *that* one, over there. In the primrose yellow.'

'Oh, that one, I see. What about her?'

'Nothing about her. That man next to her, do you see him? Wearing black?'

'Where?'

'There. You're looking straight at him.'

'In black, you say?'

'Yes.'

'Can't say as I do, old boy. Though it's difficult to see anything much with this blasted mask – it keeps slipping over my eyes. You don't mean that fellow there with the black breeches?'

'No, all in black. Look, he's over there now. Just moving behind the woman in the red dress.'

'I can't see anyone.'

'No, you can't see him now.'

'What about him? Did you recognise him? Was he someone famous?'

'No, I just noticed him and wondered if you had. It was his costume, I suppose,' I added lamely. 'Being all in black like that.'

'Hmm. Funny sort of choice for a ball if you ask me, black. Give me a colour any day. I think this old Harlequin get-up's rather fine, don't you? Though where I shall wear it when we get home I don't know.'

I looked at Henry's drooping figure attired in its varicoloured finery and tried to envisage the picture recreated in the sober surroundings of Musford Park. Inwardly, I quailed.

'Where's George, anyway?' I asked, changing the subject.

'He went to ask some girl to dance, I think. Yes, there he is.' Henry pointed, but it took me some time to pick out George's lanky figure over the other side of the ballroom. Maybe it wasn't so odd that Henry hadn't been able to spot my man in black. There were enough people here, after all. And perhaps I had been mistaken in my earlier impression that no-one saw him but me. I mean, I had to be, the whole idea was ridiculous. Anyway, I couldn't see him myself now, so I allowed Henry to lead me in the direction of the wine. Never at my ease in gatherings of strangers, I found that finding a drink at least gave one the feeling of being profitably occupied.

We made our way over to the serving tables, pushing through the crowd. It was strange how the wearing of a mask affected one. I felt it myself, the heightened excitement, the feeling of being a step removed from one's everyday personality. The sense of licence.

'Are you going to dance?' I asked Henry, once we were each supplied with alcohol.

'I suppose one should. You?'

'I imagine it will be hard to avoid,' I said. 'Besides, we are intending, are we not, to make the acquaintance of certain Venetian ladies?'

Indeed, we had talked of little else for weeks. We had read, before we embarked on our travels, of the delights of the women of Venice. One writer had described them as 'peculiarly bewitching'. Reading between the lines, it was hinted that their fame was not only for their style and beauty – though these were legendary – but also for, shall we say, their skills in other directions. Suffice it to say, Tibbs had not been at all happy to let us out alone.

Tibbs was Henry's tutor, our bearleader on our travels or, to put it more plainly, our nursemaid. He was only a few years older than us, though you wouldn't have thought it. Poor Tibbs was a dull old stick. To be fair, he had an unenviable task. Our goal was experience, whatever the cost. Our worthy parents, however, desired that we both improve our minds and not too heavily deplete their wallets. Such conflicting aims meant that we were frequently required to give Tibbs the slip and, indeed, were not above adding a purging powder to his coffee if we desired an evening free of his restraining influence.

This evening, however, happily for us, Tibbs had most obligingly succumbed to a sick headache of his own accord, leaving us eager to encounter all that life had to offer. And now here we were, loose in the Venetian night with all its scented and painted wonders spread before us.

We stood watching the patterns made as the dancers turned, crossed and turned again. There was certainly plenty on which to feast the eye, for the scene was one of magnificent ostentation. The ballroom was lined with mirrors so that innumerable chandeliers appeared to stretch away into infinite distance. Above, the ceiling was an elaborate confection of cherubs and clouds, while any inch of the room that was not painted or mirrored was gilded and scrolled. To English eyes, the effect was unspeakably vulgar, yet it could not be denied that it had a certain *bravura*. One side of the room was taken up with huge windows stretching from the floor almost to the ceiling; these stood open in an attempt to relieve the heat. The unmistakable smell of canals that haunts one wherever one goes in Venice entered on the night air, fetid and rank.

It was true that the women were magnificent, and they knew it. To compare them to Englishwomen was like comparing sparrows with peacocks. Despite my earlier *braggadocio,* to speak truth, I couldn't imagine daring to ask one to dance. They carried themselves with such confidence, so different from the girls one met at the county balls at home. Of course, not all Englishwomen were country misses, but the Venetian *belladonnas* outclassed any woman I had seen. Their dresses were the colours of jewels, rich and glowing, and the fabric was stiff with gilt thread and lace. Nor had they skimped on gems: each white throat rose from a wirework collar where gleamed rubies, sapphires, emeralds. Who cared if the precious stones were paste? The effect was all and the effect was magnificent.

The dance was coming to an end; the music built to a conclusion and ended in a flourish. Facing each other in two long lines, the dancers bowed and curtsied to their partners. A ripple of applause broke through the assembly.

Henry turned to me. 'Should we take that as our cue?' I must have looked blank, for he went on. 'To ask someone to dance, I mean!' His dear silly face was lit with enthusiasm.

'I suppose so,' I said, trying to quell the butterflies that took flight in my stomach at the very idea.

'Come on then.' Placing his empty glass on the tray of a server, who had most obligingly appeared at that moment, Henry set forth into the fray. Downing the remnant of my drink, I, too, deposited my glass and prepared to do battle.

Henry, I saw, was approaching a group of young women and I thought I could do worse than join him. After all, there were four of them. Just as Henry had drawn close, however, a horde of Italians bore down on the girls and carried them off from under his nose.

I joined Henry's side. 'Perhaps we will have better luck over there.' I steered him towards a couple of women standing near, affecting a boldness I did not feel, for to my mind, they were far above our touch.

It seemed they thought so too, for in response to my stammered Italian they raised two pairs of carefully painted eyebrows, exchanged a complicit look and swept away to where two men, older and infinitely more sophisticated than ourselves, were waiting for them.

'Third time lucky, perhaps,' I muttered in Henry's direction.

All the most delectable specimens appeared to have been snapped up by this stage, leaving us with the Venetian equivalent of the wallflower. Still, one had to start somewhere, and at least these girls might not snub us. We approached a pair standing together. I made my bow, murmured 'Vuoi ballere con me?' and she took my outstretched hand. Henry had equal success, and the two of us bore our partners out into the centre of the ballroom.

That became the first dance of many that evening and we found, once we hit our stride, that the English milord was not unsort-after by the local ladies. More than one eye was flashed in our direction or fan fluttered. Yet I found myself distracted. Even as we danced, my eyes roved the room, searching for another glimpse of that mysterious man in black. Perhaps, behind the mask, he was indeed someone famous – Lord Byron, maybe, for he was rumoured to be still in Venice. The charisma that had drawn my eye was surely the assurance of a man celebrated wherever he went, either for talent or worldly position. And yet, I reminded myself, no-one else seemed even to have noticed him, much less been as struck by him as I had.

It was around the tenth dance of the evening when it happened. I was partnering a dark-haired woman in a dress of vivid green. A few short months ago, I would have been flabbergasted to imagine myself here, in company with such beauty. And yet I felt curiously absent, as if my body and only my body performed these motions, while my spirit was elsewhere, questing restlessly.

My partner and I clasped hands, circled. I passed her on to the next gentleman in line, taking the hand of another lady in her turn. And then

I saw him, the man in black. He was in the dance, further down, moving up the line towards me. And he seemed to be looking straight at me.

I stopped dead as if I had been struck. Only when other bodies passed between us, cutting off the intensity of that gaze, did I realise that I was motionless, the dance around me broken up into confusion.

'Mi scusi, per favour, mi non bene. Not well,' I added, feeling my Italian deserting me. I blundered out of the dance, clutching my hand to my head.

Indeed, I did not feel well. How was it that this man had such an effect on me? Was I going out of my mind? Thankful for the mask that sheltered me from curious glances, I retreated to the side of the room. Yet my sanctuary was disrupted by the sight of a strange figure who loomed up before me. In his hired costume and mask, it was a moment before I recognised him as myself, reflected in the mirrored wall. Even then, his pale countenance seemed not my own.

Hastily, I turned my back. I must compose myself. If only I could be sure that the man in black was real, that others saw him too. I searched up and down the line of dancers. The whirling colours confounded the eye, making a mockery of any attempt to isolate a single figure. Yet no matter how hard I stared, I saw no sign of him.

I was shaking, I realised, my skin covered with a cold sweat. It was no wonder. The room was stifling – I needed air. I pushed my way through the crowd.

The evening was so still that hardly a breath of air entered through the tall windows. Stepping out, I found that they gave onto a balcony which ran the width of the house. Even here, I could not be alone, but had to squeeze between packed bodies, passing through clouds of tobacco smoke and a gabble of Italian. I crossed to the balustrade. If I could not see anyone, I could pretend I was by myself.

I untied my mask, wiped my face with my handkerchief. My hands were still trembling. I felt in my pockets for my cigar case. A smoke would steady my nerves. A lantern had been left burning on the balcony, perhaps with the intention of providing a light for the tobacco-lovers amongst us. I was grateful, for it saved me accosting someone. I trimmed the end of the cigar, held it in the flame, turning it so that it burned evenly. I drew on it, concentrating all my attention on the ember, the way it glowed and then died with each breath. The taste and smell of my Turkish tobacco was comfortingly familiar.

A gondola passed below, the lantern at its prow throwing a circle of gold on the dark water. The splash of the oars and the boat's creak came to me. Other lights reflected their image too. Here and there, burning torches flared, lighting the flights of steps that led up from the water. The fires gave the scene a touch of the infernal. I was reminded of a medieval wall-painting I had once seen in a country church, miles from anywhere – a depiction of the horrors of hell, in which demons tormented their victims at numerous small fires very much like those I saw before me.

I smiled at my fancy. It had been a long summer, full of novel experiences. Perhaps my mind was rebelling at the wonder, the strangeness of it all. Was it anything to marvel at if the beauty of Venice turned the mind a little? Did any Englishman return to his shire entirely untouched? The whole city, after all, was an eternal pageant, gloriously coloured. There was nothing in that to inspire dismay. And if the masks and costumes, the gilt and mirrors, the heat and the crowds had conspired to make me feel for a moment a trifle unbalanced, then what of it? I would not be the first to find the ballroom oppressive, and we were in Italy, in the heat of the summer.

The ember of my cigar flared and died, flared and died, mirroring the flickering torches. When I had finished my smoke, I would return to the ballroom and find George and Henry. Supper would put me to rights, I told myself, though in truth I felt little enough like eating.

Lovely as Venice was, I suddenly wished myself far from here, far from the crowds and the smells. I imagined some enchanted woodland glade, a ruined tower perhaps, lit by moonlight, and the scent of jasmine on the soft air. A nightingale would be singing from a nearby thicket and the stars, the eternal stars that had watched over Cicero, would burn in the sky overhead as they would to the end of time.

I do not know what it was that told me. A movement, perhaps, or a sound? Whatever it might have been, I found my every sense suddenly alive. The skin at my back prickled, as if I was being watched. Perhaps George or Henry had followed me. Yet my flesh knew it was neither George nor Henry who stood there. Slowly, I turned.

It was the man in black. He stood leaning against the balustrade, his back to the panorama of the Grand Canal, regarding me steadily. Even from behind the mask, his eyes seemed to burn. The force of that gaze transfixed me, holding me captive. Suddenly aware that I had removed my mask, I was conscious of a feeling of nakedness, of exposure. Neither of us spoke – I doubt my lips could have formed words. Then his mouth lifted in a smile and his face was transformed, as if lit from within.

The Anchorite's Tale

Charlotte Symons

(A short story)

The sun at this time of year is low. It slants through the narrow window into the cell, charting her hours with the movement of its light. Every day, she watches its passage. Today she has moved her stool a few inches so that the sun falls on her body, clothed in its dark habit. She rolls back the sleeves, lets her pale skin soak up its gold. The warmth enters her like the presence of God, slowly making Himself known. The light of the world. To those who were in darkness.

Even now, after a decade of confinement, her mind is rebellious. The little things, those that should lead her to contemplation of her God and His wonders, instead these lead her astray, down paths of the flesh. Now, the sun on her skin brings to mind certain times. Once in particular – that first time, by the secret pool. They had found it one day caught high in the hills, like a dew-drop in a leaf. So cold, the icy-fingered water ringing her legs, first her ankles, then her calves, thighs, making her gasp. And then, afterwards, lying on soft moss while the sun played its warmth over her; the breeze, its breath.

She should pray, pray for forgiveness for these thoughts that still afflict her, pray for the strength to resist. Pray to be delivered from them? No, never that.

But she should pray, always, she should pray, sending her prayers spinning skywards. For she is the anchorite, her vocation to anchor the church to heaven with her devotions. She imagines it sometimes, pictures herself floating far above the earth, a spider on a thread of gossamer high in the blue air.

Sometimes at night she dreams she can fly. So real, then to wake and find them false. Outside the window the apple tree is bare. Only the mistletoe hangs green in the skeleton branches. In the midst of death we are in life.

It was the summer before last she first saw the girl, meeting her lad after church under that tree. The girl's clothes were poor and drab, but her hair was a glowing chestnut. They must have thought they would not be seen at this end of the building, out of sight of the main door. They forgot the anchoress in her cell. Once she saw them kiss, felt for an instant such longing.

Later, the girl was on her own, picking apples in the dawn. She was thin, her bare arms like the bones of a bird. She never looked over to where another woman watched.

When she saw the girl again, her belly was large under a ragged gown. Before the anchorite knew what she was doing, she had called to the girl through the unshuttered window.

The sound of her own voice shocked her; she clapped a hand to her mouth, wishing she could call it back, stuff the cry down her rebellious throat. She took a step back from the window, her heart clamouring.

It was not her role to initiate contact with those outside. Her vocation was prayer and only prayer, and she was maintained by the church for that purpose. Even her bread was not hers to give away, but was given by others to sustain her in her work.

Her bread. She had some left from the midday meal. In recent days, she had been feeling low in spirits as the dusk drew near and had taken to keeping a piece of bread to eat at such moments.

The girl was still there, standing uncertain under the tree, an Eve without an Adam. She would not see the anchorite, clothed as she was in the darkness of her cell. Again, she called out and this time reached her arm across the thickness of wall that divided them so that she could thrust the bread through the narrow window.

'Take it,' she said, as the girl drew near. But perhaps she had misjudged. Perhaps the girl was not in need and would be insulted by her charity.

But the girl came closer, until she could see her only in fragments. Eyes too large in a face smudged with shadows. The girl reached for the bread, fingertips brushing hers. The touch sent a jolt of – what was it? – through her to the core. It was the first time she had touched another human hand in ten years.

The anchorite snatched her hand away, catching it on the stonework so that it stung. It might as well have been the girl's touch that caused such stinging. She held her hand to her chest, nursing it, her heart fluttering like that of a bird, caught in the net and trembling.

✦

The next day she kept her bread and her soup, ignored the mutterings of her stomach. She was used to fasting. Between Prime and Terce, between the prayer times of Sext and None, she watched. As she sat at her Lectio Divina, she found herself, every few minutes, glancing up from the book and wondering.

The girl came as evening was dropping toward dusk. A whispered word outside the window that made the anchorite start from her stool. She picked up the bowl of soup, her hands unsteady. This time she pushed the bowl to the window, handed out the spoon so that the girl could feed herself by reaching in through the stonework. The girl's hands shook so that she spilt much of the soup, knocking the spoon against the window-surround. When the bowl was empty, the anchorite gave her the bread. Their fingers touched. Again, the jolt that ran through her to the core, the feeling that was like unto God. Such blasphemy.

After that the girl had come for many days, until the anchorite grew faint with fasting. Then one day the girl did not come. The dusk closed in, the thrush flew to roost from his perch in the apple, and still she did not come. The soup, long cold, sat in its wooden bowl on the stool by her side. Sick with hunger, she waited. The girl might still come under cover of darkness. Her stomach growled. She sank to her knees to pray.

*

In the grey light of morning she ate. In a few hours she would be brought more and she could save that instead. As she waited she wondered what had happened, if it was time for her to be brought to bed. She thought not, that her belly was not yet large enough, but she knew she was not wise in such things. Remembering, she tries again to imagine it, swelling like a fruit with new life. Yet she cannot regret her choice – there are other matters, rich and strange, which she would never have known were it not for the womb of these four walls.

The days passed. She did not see the girl again. Never even knew her name. Had she moved on, found work and a place to stay? Or was she dead, her child cold in her unliving womb? For months, the thought of her was a nagging ache. The anchorite never asked, not having a name to give to the face. But the girl haunted her, those thin features, still touched with the breath of youth.

The Lord, in His infinite wisdom, knows. Yet how can He bear it, so many souls in their pain? She had thought when she entered the anchorhold that here was a refuge from the storms of the world. She was young then, too young to have learnt that the torment of the heart will follow wherever goes the flesh. Even from this narrow window she can see the gibbet on the hill, the bodies blown by the wind, their souls known only to God. Over the years, she has come to know that all the world is here, in this stone-encompassed room. (She can pace it out – four paces this way, four paces that.) Here she has known the heights of despair and the deepest joy. She has sent her prayers spinning into the void and felt them climb to the light. Feared there was no God and known that there was. Watched the turning of the year as the apple-tree changed with the seasons. The apple that was the tree of knowledge and the tree of life, the tree of Adam and of Golgotha. The tree where the lovers met, where the girl plucked fruit.

The anchorite shifts on her stool. The winter sun has rolled round in its orbit while she has been sitting and the light now falls, a spear of gold, on the stone floor, pointing the way to the crucifix on the wall. The man of sorrows, who suffers all, endures all. She turns back her sleeves so they once more cloak her pale flesh with their dark fabric. It is time for her offices. Later, when darkness has fallen, she will eat her bread.

Once she is sure the girl will not come this day.

Waiting (to Haunt)

Alick McCallum

Opening Thoughts from a Manifesto

Forgive me for any gross assumptions; I have too few words to play with. I have learnt that spectres leave, remain and arrive without ever having been present, and it is these spectres I propose here.

In life there are certain pieces of art that occupy a black space behind your eyes, works that invariably situate themselves so honestly within your self that you cannot re-locate them until your eyes are re-introduced to their original. I call out for personal reference: Miro's *Maternity*, Rothko's *Number 18*, Dali's *The Persistence of Memory* and Malevich's *Black Square*, and I would like to also call out Gupta's sculpture *From Far Away Uncle Moon Calls* and his painting *The Beach* which somehow domesticated me within Malevich's *Black Square*. Works such as these inhabit a spectral moment within you. I do not believe that the sensations they arouse ever exist. I believe only that the works arouse you momentarily into an awareness of a spectral void in which the work of art and the self exist outside temporal bounds, innately and unconsciously in equilibrium with each other. When you encounter these pieces of art you are unconscious and you are haunted.

Now to writing. I come to writing knowing it to be a ghost, but conscious that it has never been, for me at least, spectral. The unexpected inevitability of Spicer's line breaks, the collected truth of Pound's apparitions and the insular exteriority of Williams' red wheelbarrow are each undeniable. I could not see life without them. But without the art referenced above, I could not feel death. No writing has reduced me so explicitly to unconsciousness as Dali's paint and so it is to that end I write; beyond words, for words too, are haunted.

If so many writers have thus far failed to arouse that explicit state of unconsciousness through their writing, why should we succeed? The reason does not lie in the quality or beauty of writing, but the mode of writing. We propose a mode of writing that falls through the so called 'forms', [prose, poetic prose, prose poetry, verse] projecting to the reader a succession, a procession even, of diffusive images to pass across the ephemeral membrane of the unconscious. For it is the unconscious, that location inherent of existence, that we journey towards. The writing becomes a dream, a spectre of the unconscious, brought out of simple manifestation into invisible latency only through unconscious consumption of the writing by the reader.

A procession of images – this is what we write and we do so to repulse the conscious. Through the perceived impossibility of the images, through the amalgamation of dichotomous and contrasting images, through an apparent fragmentary cohesion to the narrative procession of the images – through these, the writing becomes a dream. The conscious, which we propose works towards interpretation and understanding, becomes confused and disorientated by the speed at which the images displace and overlap each other. Much like it does to a dream on waking, the conscious rejects the images.

The writing is rejected, discarded from the conscious. Having been irrevocably consumed, it falls into a spectral state in which, to the conscious mind, it is both yet to happen, has already happened and never will happen. The writing, occupying a black space beside the conscious, cannot disappear and cannot reappear and so unnoticed, as the spectre it has become, diffuses into and remains in the unconscious as a negation of manifestation, as a blooming of latency, in equilibrium with the unconscious it now haunts. The haunting of the words leaves and remains and arrives, without ever having been present.

The writing that follows cannot claim to fulfil all the ambitions set out above, but is a first pursuit of those ambitions. It is the beginning of a longer body of writing that aims to discover the spectral in itself.

Both the manifesto and the writing are to be extended.

*

Waiting (to Haunt)

(Ink

      Paint

)

Only the dripping of colour, violet through a yellow ocean, three rivers through a lake, one colour from each current an oil spill in fresh water at the shore of a nuclear meadow. Blades of grass –

    fluorescent green
        (
        evergreen trees)
              separated
                     from white walls
                        no black lines
                            no distance

        colour:shade:gap:bridge

              the world
              in the eyes that see it

I close mine again and see:

A crocus emerging from the western
peak of an amniotic sac caught within the temporal stasis of a spring
blooming womb. The crocus oscillates between a space sanctified
by purple and green and the crocus flowers and grows and flowers
and grows until the atomic translucency of the peak dissipates in
a perpetual motion of pollination. Purple leaves impregnate green
pedicels and the offspring dissipate into an amnesiac prism, a shadow
where green forgets grass and purple forgets, slowly begins to fray

at the eye
of a crocus

the spine
down the flower

is cut open
falls apart

Sap oozes from the tear and at each
side the flowerhead droops along the arc of gravity. Bulbous sap throbs
along the stamen, pools at the anther as a sticky weight. Gravity arrives
in the same colour as wind and the crocus weeps for its own death

sap
is a globule
stuck still in air

remembers
seconds ago in an ovary

sap falls
like rain
like tears

silent   tears   it apart

sap, like everything that falls,

waits to become
a mushroom

The sap impacts,
becomes indistinguishable, remains present only as an unseen
mushroom eruption micrometres above a soil bed, fructose dispensed
at a molecular level to numerous potential salad bowl

Waiting (to Haunt)

a garden

waiting

to become

At some point under the soil surface a piece of crocus is stripped of
its past, remains unconditionally ephemeral in a vesicatory passage
towards

chopped cucumber
sellotaped together
and too much

between segments   not enough
            fruit in the bowl

            Except plums, a waterfall of ripe
plums over a ceramic ridge into a moist river bed splashes juice
through cracked skin into a run of blue sugar

Moonshine

cold blue river (cleaves before breath)

gasps

and (red water falls
in one fall
)

a slow nosebleed trail down to the tip.
(pirouettes   off nipple)

drip.

(pool of red
pools red
in red pool
)

into iris   (red confluence   [a blue hollow pool]

ravine artery.

a blink   )

Awakened, an eye sees itself in colour as red coagulates with green, grass cuts through blood, brown fumes erupt. A worm slices through it all and disintegrates into dust. Red, green and brown moths flutter into the sky and brown clouds hang in a yellow backdrop. The world returns to primary

colour

      :

           language

               :

                  latitudes

                     :

                         location - x

                      A rainbow diffuses
across the membrane of another rainbow, twin bands of light paralysed beneath

          breaking clouds –

          – photons meet

          in vitro

At the location
of a centre perpendex photons equilibrate into a frothy translucency
in the shape of letter x. Light, cooled from colour and frozen as image,
turns into a water veil hovering in the sky

first honey   spring's final
    collected   lily blooms
        beneath hive   into flower

        rainbow quakes on a pond
        between lives of water

        pinecone   bumblebee
    reflection gone   sting remains
before   after

Light returning from infinite latitudes and longitudes meets at the
epicentric rainbow and flashes photons as still scenes

Waiting (to Haunt)

x
is a cat hooked
to a fishing line

x
is dragged back
on a single line

x
is floundering
in green waves

x
is torn
by a violet current

x
is a red blotch
on a black line

The cat is frozen, the
hook has broken its brittle flesh, ((fur, fizzing, fleeing, floating,
feathers)) has been pulled back empty to the fisherman who is
standing at x's coefficient, who is standing in a yellow anorak on the
sunny shore, who is sweat dripping into his hood, who is sweat filling
his boots to the brim.

The cat melts, the man melts, the anorak is stoic
and sails towards a large letter x. The anorak sinks. x lactates into the
wet waters. The sun shines and

                    the reflection
                    of sky
                    is milk
                    straight from
                    teat
                    gulped from
                         – areola

                    the reflection
                         of sky
                         is excrement
                         in eyes

The milky sky falls
and behind its clotted curtain – one thesis on the origin of x marks the
spot – the ejaculation of a giraffe on the bare back of a cockroach, the
heaving globules of cum strings from scales and pink foreskins to the
sandy desert floor

```
                    yellow sky
                 and brown clouds
              that nuclear meadow
       which is now purple grass and has feathers
                  – the horizon
        a
giraffe lies
  in sweat
     with
     and
     on top
      of a
       cock
       roach
      the cock
      roach spreads
     its back legs and a web of sticky lust
     strings and droops and drips and pools
    in a white pool in the belly of the desert
   the semen                  lake reflects
     the yell                   ow sky
   brown                      clouds
       are                     misty
       the        (cock        semen
      rain        roach         bow
                        s                   w
                    c   a         a
                  t             e
                  t                       a
                  r s                 y        )
```

Rising to the heads of the gloopy pair, a trumpet creeper has reached the sun

                              sun sucks
            red brass
in morning   sun blows
                  red trumpet
      at night

                        Which falls in both a figurative
and literal sense, as colour is usurped by
                              blue,
                              black blue
                              the night
                              is ice sheet –
                              soiled
                              across
                              blood salt   plain

                              salt plain,
                              salty – is cold
                              night
                              is cold

                              salt runs
                              over
                              a bed of
                              fruit

                              ice burns
                              a wet hole
                              in blue

Waiting (to Haunt)

Blue night sinks into water, deep water. The wet night sky is blue with trillions of pools contained in the spaces between hydrogen molecules, a microcosm of a micro-ecosystem where microscopic frogspawn spawn, grow, die, decompose, breath. A heron slices through gravity, cuts the sun in two, cuts between the atom and molests the micro world, catching saltwater fish odours from the ligaments of clouds

      water vapour
      sings
      about   rain   drops
                                the drum
                                on window

                        The underbelly of which briefly contains the underside of a bird. The heron from before has returned, is carnivorous, carries half a melted cat in a beak cleft open down its left-hand side.

      the cat screams in a shrill male human voice

As its melted flesh is sliced open down its spine, as its vertebrae open up in a blooming of marrow, as the marrow turns from milk to stone from stone to water

           the heron
           drinks
           the cat
           in pints

The heron reaches back and conjures forth the ceramic bowl filled with
dead sour plums. It pours the cat amongst them. The blood and skin
of fruit and mammal liquidise and drown the tapestry etched upon the
inside of the bowl

the stencil

of a woman

claws

her way

up

The pottery away

from the rising purple. Her fingers spew into magma, oozing and
solidifying on the porcelain rim, from stencil to lava, liquid to quartz,
ceramic to flesh, fire to blue

ornamental

woman

drowns

Her extra dimensional fingers break from the bowl and the heron
weeps

> tears drip
> along the birth
> of a feather
> out
> of the sky
> a cat rains
> from a bird

Verse on Spectres

Alick McCallum

Pendle Hill – Ever Home

If you set one foot before another – walk
, amble up Pendle Hill.
Fall upwards. The chalk

splayed out – the eventual anvil
of the wind's hammer, singularly vertical
in its vocabulary. "Windmill"

translated only as mathematical
terminus – epicentre
of a met[eo]rological   ""

Sideways breezes are lamented.
A funeral of ice dandelion raindrops.
Snow fauna is the sky, the scented

sky – endless from the hilltop;
the speckled mist, the sensuous sky –
the enchanted shroud, death gown

of Mother Malkin. Speckled Wood Butterflies
loft above her bones, her crown,
her temple. *Mau* is mummified

and concealed and wrapped and laid down
and consumed by stone.
Pyramidal cairns – fossilised infinite signposts

along the berth of Lancashire's great innominate bone.
A ghost
and a throne.

A carboniferous easternmost
rising. Decomposed sphagnum moss
deposit. The chill

of loss
in descent. The gradual fall of cross-county windmills
over the falling horizon. The bliss and the loss

walking and sitting with Pendle Hill.

Flotsam

a piece of flotsam
a cold chestnut
        brown blot
        in the blue

bobbing and very small

Dusk

church, bird, sing –

      expiry of bird,
expiry of stars,

chiming bell, announce
retirement of grass –
  the world of tarmac
and streetlamp moons

After Swoboda, Reflections

as much as of reflections
as of the eye
as of the trees, the lilies
as of obvious autumn
as of the water

surface ripple
undulating
temporal beyond a dropped stone

one feather quaking in a breeze
its own phantom
between lives on the water

reflections of pinecones
gone before they happened

water contains so many ghosts
lives too brief to be forgotten
remembered only as their own infinitudes

On Spectres

i

a tree drips
, the bark is green
and the leaves
have vanished
, consumed
by an empty
space

green pools
on the floor
beneath
empty leaves

between two
spaces, a kestrel flies
, an arrow
with black spots

the kestrel lands
on a colourless branch
cutting the spaces
in two

and that is where it sits
now, brown and black
and with yellow eyes

ii

if everything is dreams then, you
, spectral woman – what are you

a weaver of gaps, a bridge
between ancestral lineage
and my ever-son
yet ever to be – never

the *you*
absent of quantification
, hovering kestrel
quantifiable only as being inevitable
and inevitably somewhere

inevitable – a fracture
and the only space either side

that is you, the blink of an eye

The Falling Man

Cheryl Powell

(A novel extract)

Chapter 1

Mordecai the caretaker had the best view of the falling man. It was lunchtime, and he was outside on the bench, packed lunch balanced on his stocky knees, sharp wind in his face. He was fumbling with the greaseproof, hoping that Janice might have put by a slice of that boiled gammon from Hopwood's, or beef with mustard. His wife could put on a damned fine spread when she was in the mood. Homemade cake, sometimes.

The man was on top of the tower block, right on the edge of the flat roof and he seemed to be limbering up, shaking his arms, as though about to walk out onto a high diving board.

Looking up, Mordecai frowned. Only he, the caretaker, was allowed up there. It was dangerous.

The man fell.

It's a funny thing, but afterwards, even years later, Mordecai was never able to touch greaseproof paper, feel its cold glossy texture, without remembering that day, though at the time, of course, greaseproof was the last thing on his mind. For as the man fell, Mordecai's brain was cranking into a higher-functioning mode, neurons and synapses on red alert, a voice in his head screaming. 'The bloody idiot is falling… the bloody idiot will die!'

The fall was actually more a collapse than a dive. The man's legs had simply buckled and there he was, plummeting towards the slabbed area where residents used to hang their washing.

'Coming down won't be pleasant for him,' thought Mordecai. There were seventeen floors: the top five empty and condemned, their windows boarded; the rest blooming with rusty satellite dishes, long disconnected; all coated with nearly sixty years of urban filth and grime. Nobody would want to see that close up, especially if death was the next step. Mordecai felt a twinge of shame; the place had deteriorated on his watch.

Another nanosecond of brain time passed and Mordecai noted that the falling man had reached the eleventh floor, arms and legs flailing, coat flapping like dark wings.

'He'll be regretting this,' Mordecai said aloud. 'Thinks he can fly. Silly bugger.'

Then he thought of Neal and Evelyn Jeffries who lived on that floor. Mordecai's heart lurched. He knew that Evelyn was there right now, washing and ironing executive shirts; pressing collars, cuffs, and backs and fronts, her wrists as thin as wishbones. And when this was done, she would probably iron Neal, her industrial steam iron tightly gripped, perhaps set to 'cotton' and on 'full steam', or gliding over his skin with a dry hotplate. Occasionally, depending on how dark her mood, she would club him around the head and face, or attempt to strangle him with the flex, holding him in a headlock until she tired. He never complained.

Mordecai had witnessed this violence many times, when sweeping the landing or swabbing out the lifts, glimpses through net curtains at the pressed shirts hanging like empty skins, the air swirling with steam and misery. Neal would be there in his underpants, sewing on buttons or rubbing at a stain, screwing up his good eye while the blind one stared blank, bony legs as thin as ladles.

Mordecai often saw Neal leave home in the black and gold Iron Man uniform he'd wear for pick-ups and drop-offs to the suburbs, his peaked cap covering the blisters on his ears, the burns and bruises on his scalp. Mordecai had told Neal just last week that he should call the police, said Evelyn would kill him one day, but Neal had looked away, said she was not well in the head and would probably die of their great sorrow, in any case. And, as always, Mordecai had felt the trip-hammer panic that came whenever he thought of Neal and Evelyn and that terrible summer's day just gone. He would always blame himself for their loss.

The falling man was churning the air now, legs cycling, arms pumping as he passed the ninth floor. Mordecai's brain had hit its stride, able to wonder, at some leisure, whether Snaggerstraat saw him plunge by the window. He pictured the Belgian artist, bare-chested, beard forked with dried paint, furiously hurling colour onto canvas – nude women with square breasts and enormous chins – or slumped by the window sobbing, tending a heart which, the old man wailed, was stilettoed by grief. 'Completely stillettoed,' he had sobbed often to Mordecai, who never knew what to say, but always nodded gravely.

'You like, yes?' Snaggerstraat had seen Mordecai looking at the canvases covering the walls and stacked on the floor. It was the same woman: holding flowers, drinking tea or riding a donkey but always the same face, the same square breasts, the same enormous chin. 'You take one. Choose. Please. A gift.'

'She's… lovely.' Mordecai had taken a picture at random, immediately dreading what Janice would say.

While thinking of Snaggerstraat, Mordecai's brain was also wondering whether falling from high buildings was likely to make you bilious, whether your breakfast might be forced up into your lungs and stop you breathing, and whether the man was likely to be sick on the way down. Mordecai had been a sickly child himself, and was still a martyr to his stomach even though he was almost sixty.

There wasn't long to wait now. The falling man was at the fifth floor, on the home stretch. Dinky Algarkirk might be looking out the window as he got ready, thought Mordecai. It was Friday, early finish, and Dinky was probably changing into a leather skirt and high heels, ready for his weekly lunch with 'the girls'. Mordecai got on well with Dinky; they both supported the same football team; he was a good bloke. But Mordecai had to be honest; the red lipstick and chandelier earrings were a worry. People might think Dinky was a tart.

'I've got a hot date tonight,' Dinky had told Mordecai the previous evening. Dinky was still in his pizza delivery uniform, light touch of powder and pink lipstick. 'Good Lord. I'm so excited. Terrified, actually.' Dinky had poured Mordecai a glass of prosecco and pointed to a red blouse on the back of the door. 'It's real silk. Charity shop in Newgit Street. Can you believe it? Think I'll toddle upstairs and get Evelyn to run her steam fairy over it for me, freshen it up.'

Mordecai smiled at the thought of Dinky but was interrupted by a great holler; the falling man was obviously anticipating the finale. His body was bucking, arms doing the backstroke, and then he clipped the ledge on the third floor where Myrtle the Irish woman lured pigeons with holy bread.

For a millisecond, the voice in Mordecai's head drowned out other thoughts. 'She's feeding those bloody pigeons, again!' it shouted. 'They're vermin, shitting all over the place. I keep telling her, notices everywhere! Silly cow!'

Mordecai always felt light-headed when he visited Myrtle. There were usually a couple of dead pigeons on the draining board, their innards in the sink, and she'd be plucking feathers with vigorous fingers or butchering them with a rusty knife. The blood would make his stomach swill. It seemed that it was Myrtle's destiny to concoct soups and stews that only the truly starving would ever risk. Or the unknowing homeless who sought sanctuary at St Drogo's further up Viaduct Street.

'Arrah, won't you be taking the morsel of soup with me, Mordecai?'

A few weeks back she had handed him a chipped cup. 'It will do you the world of good, so it will.'

The soup had fur in it. 'It'll bloody kill us,' Mordecai said, and had raised the alarm.

That was in early summer, when Neal and Evelyn still had Nancy and were out for a walk, leaving their soup untouched by the front door. Snaggerstraat had topped his up with flesh-tinted oil paint and was swirling the curdled mess across the heaving breasts of his next masterpiece. Most of the other residents were watching daytime telly and had left it on the doorstep. Wholesale poisoning averted, at least for now.

'Oh, but look, here's an awkward moment.' Mordecai's brain flexed a little. The man was about to land, gathering speed, a missile coming in face first. Mordecai's brain raced. 'That face will come off as soon as the man hits the deck.' He felt the contents of his stomach rise. But, thankfully, at the last second, the man flipped onto his back. Mordecai, locked in the moment, brain whirring, heard the thud as the man hit the ground, felt the vibration, saw the body jolt, then lay broken like a spent firecracker.

Mordecai stared, waiting for his breathing to start again. Involuntarily, he gazed down at his lunch, a groan surfacing as his brain registered the final affront. Fish paste sandwiches.

*

The fallen man lay on his back, for all the world sun-bathing, were it not for one crooked arm, an awkward angle of the leg and a dark halo of blood and brain spreading from his head like lumpy gravy. He'd landed no more than twenty feet from where Mordecai sat on the bench, sandwiches sliding off his knees. The corpse wore a designer coat. Mordecai could see, even without getting up, it was top-notch quality.

It couldn't be one of his residents, then. He relaxed a little. Nobody he knew.

The first straggle of people were making their way down the stairs – the lifts had been out of order for two years – and were edging their way for a closer look, silent and anticipating carnage. Ahead of them was Myrtle, her hand clamped to her mouth in shock. Galvanised, Mordecai shot up, trod on his sandwich, but kept going.

'No! Keep away, Myrtle,' he cried, trying not to look at the man's face, not wanting to see blood, staring instead at the designer label on the splayed lining of his coat: Armani. He was a toff, then. 'Don't look at the face, Myrtle,' pleaded Mordecai. 'It'll give you nightmares if you look at the face.'

But Myrtle, no stranger to nightmares, looked right at the face and held its gaze.

The man was gurning: face crumpled, lips buried somewhere inside the mouth, a toothless grin, eyes goggling.

'For the love of Jaysus, here comes the soul,' she said. 'Stand back. Don't touch it!'

Mordecai knew never to touch a soul. If you touched a soul you would have no peace from it and the soul no resting place. Kindest thing to let it go, souls evaporated quickly enough in the earth's atmosphere.

The fallen man's soul had pushed back the mouth and was squeezing itself between bloody jaws, elbowing itself over the tongue and between the teeth, wrestling as though out of a tight manhole, slippery with body fluid like some monstrous afterbirth. It stood up on wobbly legs, shaken by the violent death of its host. It was transparent and light in places, thick with growths and cactus-like tumours in others.

'I know that man,' said Myrtle. 'Poor wretch that he was. I know him.' Mordecai watched the soul slink away, dissolve, and then was gone.

'You know him?' Mordecai looked closer. Beneath the smart coat, the man wore ragged jogging bottoms and a stained sweatshirt. He looked familiar.

'It's Duggie Downes,' said Myrtle. 'One of the homeless that comes to St Drogo's. Poor Duggie was a sick man, you know. Parkinson's. May the Lord Almighty take pity on him.'

'Well, his soul is well out of it now, Myrtle,' Mordecai said, a tremble in his legs. 'It's the body we've got to deal with.'

'You'll be wanting to call the police, hand it over to them entirely,' Myrtle told him. 'But are you alright yourself, Mordecai. You look peaky about the gills, that you do.'

Mordecai tried not to stare at the blood; it brought back a bad memory, and so he looked at Myrtle in her hairy brown coat, knitted from mammoth hair by the look of it, the hem of her dress sagging below, knobbly and orange. These were the clothes she wore all the time, whether inside her freezing flat, or out.

'That soul will be making a holy show of itself in Hell before the day's out,' said Myrtle, shaking her head. 'The Devil takes great pleasure in a suicide.' And she drew a crucifix on her chest with a finger.

*

Myrtle had a particular interest in souls; she knew they were easily corrupted and that God in all his glory had too many to be going on with to let in any old eejit. Souls entirely free from mortal sin had a chance. Not her own, though. Her own soul had seen how things were going with her and legged it years ago.

'Your soul is in mortal danger, Myrtle,' her mother had chastised her as a child. 'Filthy, evil sinner that you are.' And suddenly, forty years later, Myrtle could taste again the white vinegar that her mother would force her to gargle with to purge the poisonous cuds from her tongue. 'Devil's roaring in your body, Myrtle,' her mother would refill the glass.

'Cast him out and throw yourself on the mercy of the Virgin Mary.'

Myrtle knew now that the mother was mad, the maddest bogtrotter to ever come out of Ireland. Even so, Myrtle was still a Catholic and believed her soul had been driven out by the mad bogtrotter mother, and could be anywhere.

*

Evelyn and Neal Jeffries had not seen the man fall past their window. It was just a coincidence that they came down, each with a sack of dirty shirts, heading for Bunty's Laundarama on Alyson Street.

'Stay where you are!' shouted Mordecai, coming forward. The sandwich under his shoe flapped and he tried to kick it off, but it was moulded to the tread. 'Sod it! Bastard thing!' He scraped his foot and some of it dislodged but the Jeffries were getting closer and he knew it would set them back to see the fallen man. 'Take Evelyn out the front way,' he batted them away. 'Bit of a mess here, that's all. Nothing to see. Take her away, Neal.'

Too late. They both wanted to see and came forward, tottering under the weight of their sacks. They stopped, looked down at the body.

*

Neal saw the fallen man and had an immediate flashback to when their great sorrow began.

It had been a blazing August day, the park teeming with families. Nancy had been propped up in the vintage pram that Neal had refurbished, a great swing boat on hoopla wheels that gleamed black and silver as it bounced its valuable cargo.

He remembered a jazz combo in the bandstand, Evelyn doing clappy-hands with Nancy and himself laughing at the child's joy. They had become parents late in life and Nancy, still less than a year old, was a thing of astonishment to them.

Oh, how they had photographed that child, the golden and cherished thing that she was: click-click-click went the Polaroid camera, then delight at the instant photographs of Nancy, smeared with ice cream and cute as a button in a cherry-patterned bonnet and matching dungarees. The storyboard of that catastrophic day.

It was an accident waiting to happen. The housing association was to blame and perhaps also that gormless caretaker; wasn't it his job to report hazards? But the fact was, there had been a loose window pane in one of the empty flats on the sixteenth floor. Nobody had realised until a pigeon flew into it, rocking it in its frame, unbalancing it. At the wrong moment, just as Evelyn had unfastened Nancy's bonnet and stepped back, the pane slipped its moorings and fell, swift as a guillotine, its landing softened by Nancy, her eyes uplifted and filled with wonder to see this glittering thing in flight.

At the time, Neal had only been aware of a great splashing and shimmering of glass around him, his skin pierced, blindness in one eye, blurred vision in the other, and then the caretaker besides them, crying and breathing heavily, shouting for Janice to ring for an ambulance. Yes, he remembered. The man had been shovelling off glass, moving like a creature lumbering underwater, tugging at something; seizing a red bundle. And the noise. Such noise. The great metallic percussion of shattering glass, echoing. He heard it still. Neal saw again the caretaker ripping off his shirt, trying to staunch the blood that leaked and spread from the red bundle. Neal had just stood, uncomprehending, Evelyn beside him, clutching the bonnet, not moving. And it seemed to him that they were no longer in the real world, but in another dimension, an alien place. Their world had changed forever.

Every day, Neal would relive that moment and take an inventory of the loss:

* one eye (his)
* one mind (hers)
* one irreplaceable child (theirs).

*

Evelyn looked down at the fallen man, at the blood, at the Armani coat she knew had once been Neal's, and she was silent for a long time. And then she shook her head.

'Do you know, Neal, I think we have to go home,' she said. 'I've left the iron on.'

*

By the time Snaggerstraat had hobbled down, wearing nothing but long johns, the dead man's bleeding had stopped and was beginning to congeal, gathering like dark puckered skin, his face bluish.

'Agh, must be arsehole from housing association, yes?' Snaggerstraat addressed Mordecai. Mordecai put his head in his hands.

'No,' he replied. 'Not a housing association arsehole. Not with that coat.'

Snaggerstraat had learned that this was a derogatory word but had yet to understand the British dress code for arseholes. He wanted to be able to identify an arsehole if one came looking for trouble. Mordecai had told him they were all arseholes in the housing association and would evict everyone in the block if they could.

Leaning closer to the fallen man, Snaggerstraat noticed his colour palette, crimson blood, bright with oxygen in places, drying brown and sluggish in others, purple earlobes. But it was the man's pallor that made his heart stumble; blue-white, just the way his beloved Velma had looked as she lay on the bed, her silver hair running through his fingers like water.

'Oh, Velma. Time has betrayed us, my lovely,' he had told her, smothering her limp white hand with kisses. 'Time is a common swindler, my dear,' and he had touched her crinkled eyelids, gilded blue, the lashes brittle with mascara. 'But he will not steal our eternity, dear heart. I won't let him do that.'

Every day since, Snaggerstraat had re-lived the moment he had met Velma. It was in Amsterdam, not so long ago. He had been strolling the red light district looking, not for sex – he was over eighty after all – but for forgetfulness, a distraction from loneliness and from a long and empty life. He had been married once, to a woman he never loved, or even liked, but who believed he would be a famous painter and gave him money. But he failed her, failed everyone. Not even his own mother would buy his work.

Unexpectedly, in Amsterdam, in an alley off the Roelensteeg, he had found love. He had stumbled upon Velma, selling her ancient body for sex, and supplementing her modest income by serving opium buns and cannabutter dumplings in the Gelukkig coffee shop.

He had visited that coffee shop every day, skipping over sun-glazed puddles like a child, beard trimmed, moustache waxed, his best velvet suit and waistcoat out of mothballs. There he would gaze at the raked verge of Velma's enormous chin and the square breasts straining under lace and silk and, at last, knew real love. Snaggerstraat smiled fondly to himself as he recalled how he had ordered everything and ate nothing, stumbling into the queasy streets sick, confused, and incoherent with longing.

'Marry me, Velma, or I shall die,' he had pleaded with her one day and she had accepted, as smitten as he. But, Time had come to claim her too soon, and within a month of marriage, Snaggerstraat's new wife was dead.

'I knew nothing of love before you,' he had told Velma, as she stiffened on the counterpane, dead from nothing more irksome than old age, her soul slipping gently from her lips. 'Now, at least I have known joy,' he said, touching the fingers of the soul, an instant before it evaporated. 'Thank you, dear heart.'

*

'Out of the way, Snaggerstraat,' Mordecai flapped his hands. 'Stop gawping at the poor bastard. Myrtle, take the old fella home and give him a bowl of your dead-dog soup, or whatever you've got.'

'I've got some of the badger stew left.'

'That'll do.'

'And some bread blessed by Father Quinn.'

Mordecai felt a small dart of annoyance. Father Quinn, the old gargoyle. 'Be sure it doesn't choke the poor bugger,' he said.

Myrtle took Snaggerstraat by the arm. He was bare-chested, shivering and tearful. 'Let's get away from this poor destroyed man,' she said. 'There's nothing we can do for him. And, besides, what would Velma say if she could see the ruin of you, out here in nothing but your nether garments?'

Mordecai watched Myrtle lead Snaggerstraat away and then unzipped his cardigan, draping it over the fallen man's face. The other residents drifted off, nothing more to see.

Then Dinky turned up. 'Just seen Janice; she's dialled 999,' he said.

'Thank God you're here, Dinky,' said Mordecai. He didn't want to be left on his own with the deceased. He was just the caretaker; he mowed the grass and cleaned the public areas and reported repairs to the housing association. He shouldn't be expected to deal with fallen men.

'Has anybody given him the kiss of life?' asked Dinky. He was in a short leather skirt and black thigh boots. Better legs than most women, thought Mordecai.

'Kiss of life? Are you kidding? Too late for that, Dinky.' Mordecai thought about the gurning corpse under the cardigan and shuddered.

'You should never give up until a doctor pronounces him dead.' Dinky put a hand on his hip.

'Believe me, Dinky, the man's dead.'

Dinky passed his clutch bag from one manicured hand to another. 'You hear of people surviving such falls.'

'Not this one,' Mordecai shook his head. 'We saw his soul leave. It's gone.'

*

Dinky wasn't going to tell Mordecai, but he had some experience of falling men. He, himself, had once been a falling man, a young man, caught wearing his big sister's undies and couldn't live with the humiliation of it. He had been fourteen.

'What in Christ's name...?' His father had come back to the house unexpectedly and barged in on him. He was parading in Trixie's girdle, stockings and a brassiere padded with socks. He was just pulling on her white patent leather boots.

His father's hand had slammed hard against his head, first one side, then the other until his ears buzzed, and then he had held him by the shoulder, looking him up and down with genuine disgust. 'Are you one of those homosexuals that are all the fashion these days?' His father had looked at him with repugnance. 'One of those poofters are you?' Turning him around. 'Well not in this family. There have never been any homosexuals in the Algarkirk family and we go back eleven generations. I'll not be having one now. Do you understand?'

Dinky could never have explained to his father that, as far as he could tell, he wasn't a homosexual; he just liked wearing girls' clothes. It was a compulsion, a need, like eating. He didn't fancy boys. Or did he? There were only boys at his boarding school and he did particularly like Alistair McCann but that was because he was funny. It was Alistair that had nicknamed him Dinky, because he was so tall. It was a joke. His real name was Jeremy. What if Alistair found out he dressed up in girls' clothes? As Dinky saw it then, there was only one way out and that was to throw himself from his bedroom window, impale himself on the spiked finial of the porch below, and die a horrible death. It would be all his father's fault. As it was, Dinky missed the finial but hit the stone lion outside the front entrance, sustaining multiple injuries. He might have died if Perkins the cook hadn't rushed out to give him the kiss of life and shoehorn his soul back down his throat.

Dinky looked again at the fallen man. 'You see, Mordecai, he might just be alive,' he said.

'Believe me, Dinky, he isn't.'

'Just possible,' Dinky held on.

'You wanna give him the kiss of life? Help yourself then.' Mordecai bent down and lifted the cardigan.

'Oh, fuck!' Dinky fainted.

Notes on the Writers

Christian Deery heralds from the Warwickshire town of Rugby, the birthplace of Rupert Brooke, the game of rugby, and a unique pronunciation of the word 'one'. His love of creating began when he realised he could earn merits for coming up with the best titles for stories in English classes. His favourite book is *In Cold Blood* by Truman Capote, and he aspires to the writing of Chuck Palahniuk and Roald Dahl. Whilst he has been touted as 'funny' by some, he has been warned that biographies are 'not the place to be funny' (quote mildly fabricated), so he will leave that to his creative pieces.
gingertelli@me.com

Thea Etnum is a linguist, art historian, photographer and an aspiring writer. It took her two undergraduate degrees, some inspirational traveling, a few extreme moments and a lot of (self)-observation to see that reality could sometimes use a bit of fiction-(alising), and that she could be one of those to do just that, through writing. She is constantly trying to shape and reshape her close, yet challenging friendship with words through every piece of fiction that she writes. It is all work in progress, and she hopes that her stories will eventually mean as much to others as they do to her.
theothereden@yahoo.com

Steve Gay writes science fiction novels and thrillers as well as short stories. He returned to university for the Warwick Writers Programme after a career in financial services. His current project is a historical novella set in his home town of Rugby during the Battle of Britain.

'*Awakening*' is the first chapter of a completed science fiction novel *The Callista Alignment*.
StephenGay@virginmedia.com

Susannah Heffernan is an emerging writer of literary speculative fiction. Her short stories pose questions of identity, alienation, and alternative realities. She has performed her work at London's Southbank Centre as part of the 2016 Festival of Love, QueerCircle at Limewharf, and at the Albany Theatre's Hothouse salon. Susannah lives in Deptford and is working on her first novel - an 'underworld quest' narrative, influenced by Dante and T. S. Eliot. If she had a time machine, she would jump in and visit Philip K. Dick and Virginia Woolf.
sueheffwrites@gmail.com

Alick McCallum was born in Burnley and remained there throughout his school years. He had numerous affairs in that time, as Pendle Hill, Trees and Poetry each led him astray from his one true love, Burnley Football Club. He completed his undergraduate degree on the Warwick Writing Programme and was kindly allowed to return for his MA. It was there that he discovered his passion for Modernist poetry, art and critical theory and is readying an essay on Denise Levertov's use of parenthesis for journal publication. Alick writes poetry and fiction and is intrigued by writing's unexplored possibilities. He is interested in mixed-media poetry and is acutely aware of his embarrassing email address.
alickthings@gmail.com

Alexander Musleh is an aspiring writer and poet who was born in Dublin in 1990 to a Palestinian Father and a Russian Mother. His multicultural background greatly affected his literary interests as well as his writing. Alexander grew up in Bethlehem, witnessing first-hand the political turmoil that plagued the Middle East. Which in turn, led him to write and explore the works of authors such as Orwell, Asimov, Maalouf, and others. Prior to undertaking his Masters at Warwick, Alexander was teaching Intensive English and working as a Communications Officer at Bethlehem University, where he hopes to return to teach full-time upon the completion of his MA.

muslehalexander@gmail.com

Cheryl Powell is a member of Solihull Writers Workshop. Her short stories have been published in *Litro*, *Everyday Fiction* and *Spelk* and in the anthologies *Rattles Tales*, published as part of the Brighton Prize 2015, and Breaking the Surface, part of the South Wales short story competition 2015. She writes about people who are misfits, creating tales that are dark with an edge of humour. *The Falling Man* is a novel-in-progress – her first.

cheryl.powell@btinternet.com

Missy Reddy was involved in many creative pursuits in her childhood; music, dancing, drama and writing. Having studied Psychology at University, she has always had a strong passion for social justice and for many years worked in services supporting vulnerable groups. Becoming a mum brought Missy back to her creative routes as she started to write stories for her own children. She writes both fiction and non-fiction and is currently writing a novel about a pregnant woman's experiences in the workplace.

missyreddy99@gmail.com

Katyana Rocker-Cook stayed on at Warwick University for the MA Writing course following her graduation from the English Literature and Creative Writing course, and is pursuing a career in screenwriting. She has written a psychological thriller entitled Walking Shadow, and more recently, has undertaken the adaptation of Marlowe's *Doctor Faustus* for television. Her passion for filmed media influences her prose through the focus on dialogue and the relationships between central characters, and she has greatly enjoyed working with the prose medium for this anthology. When she's not writing, Katyana can be found re-reading *Great Expectations*, or belting out show tunes whilst attempting to bake. *krockercook@gmail.com*

Kurt Shead was born in 1991 in Leamington Spa. He fell in love with books at an early age after reading *The Hobbit*. His first novel, *Able*, was self-published in 2013. He is also the lead script writer for *Tower Bridge Films,* a film production company based in Warwickshire and Los Angeles. When he is not reading and writing, Kurt enjoys the theatre, daydreaming, music, sleep, chocolate or any pleasurable combination of the above.

Kurt loves his family. He owes them far too much. He is currently a Masters student at the University of Warwick.
kurt.shead@gmail.com

Charlotte Symons began life in the Cotswolds, but for the last twenty years has been based in Wales. After leaving school at fourteen, she went to university in her twenties and now has a degree in English Literature with a specialism in the medieval and Renaissance periods. She finds inspiration for her own writing in the literature of the past, as well as in myths and folk tales and the beautiful countryside of the Powys/Herefordshire borders. Genres and authors that she particularly enjoys include Victorian sensation novels and the Decadent period, especially the works of Oscar Wilde, and the uncanny stories of M. R. James and Robert Aickman.
csymons1@outlook.com

Beth L. Thompson is a writer of fiction and poetry. She works as a freelance writer in Birmingham and is an MA student at the University of Warwick where she is working towards the completion of her first novel. Beth was born and raised in Liverpool where she grew up dancing,